1

The Grand Palace saloon right in the middle of the growing mining town of Peralta, catered to the great (if anyone great ever actually came through town), near great, ranchers and fifteen-dollars-a-month cowboys who could rub elbows with men of a different breed. Edward Chambers and Rolo Mackenzie were not cowboys. Far from it. The two were businessmen who resembled unmatched book ends. Chambers stood an even six feet tall, roundly built, with a ruddy-faced complexion topped by a shock of curly red hair. Mackenzie was a full half foot shorter, almost boney in appearance, with thinning black hair even though he was only thirty years old and dark, penetrating eyes.

Both had come to Peralta with enough money to begin quietly buying up old gold mining claims which the owners had either abandoned or were convinced were played out. Those pick-and-shovel prospectors were at least half right. The wrong half. The first sudden discovery of gold that started a rush to the timber-lined community gave Peralta its first shout of notoriety. But the shout turned into a mere whisper when surface gold proved too little and too far between. When the easy surface colour was cleaned up in creeks and streams, a few diehards who hung on to their claims went down into quartz-hard ground with hand tools, dynamite, sweat and broken backs trying to find a new source of yellow iron. They never did. Chambers and Mackenzie began their selective buying spree with two things in abundance: a quiet determination to purchase as many claims as possible, and a thorough education in mining geology. They knew the thick grey sludge cussed by the miners that had been clogging up rockers and box riffles was actually high-grade silver ore most others had no knowledge of. While people laughed at the worthless ground the two were buying up, the mine men felt they were on the trail of a fabulously rich mother-load of silver, one they thought might rival the mighty Comstock Lode.

This evening both men worked late in their office going over paperwork and mining claims maps. Finishing late, they decided to have a quick drink before going home even though it was not their habit to stop at the Grand Palace. It was just a convenient few doors down from their office, so they stepped inside.

'I'll have a brandy,' Chambers ordered as the barkeep, a bald-headed man with thick black sideburns and an enormous handlebar moustache, nodded, reaching under the counter.

'Make it two.' Rolo held up a pair of fingers.

'You do wash the glasses, don't you?' Chambers half kidded the server.

'Inside and out,' he replied, pouring two brandies from a new bottle. 'I'll leave it up top in case you two gentlemen want a second.'

At the end of the bar, four brothers leaned on the big oaken top watching the mine men in disgust. Their rough, heavily bearded faces, threadbare clothes and mud-splattered boots made it clear they were not men of wealth, position, or had ever been close to either one. In fact the Goss brothers, Elwood, Virgil, Emmett and Ike, had a reputation for being the exact opposite. They rarely talked to anyone in town except family members, viewing everyone else with dark suspicion. The entire family held a special hatred of the way Chambers and Mackenzie had suddenly come into town buying up most of the land around their dilapidated horse and cow ranch. Just one canyon over, the mine men had sunk a new shaft so close they could hear the muffled thud of dynamite and sometimes even feel the ground shake beneath their feet.

Their father, Vernal, was crippled for life in an accident when the brake on a heavy freight wagon he was working on gave way, the wheels running over him, crushing both legs. He had to be lifted by the boys every morning out on the front porch, placed in a chair with a heavy blanket over his legs. He'd howl and cuss every time another dynamite charge went off. If Vernal was demanding and mean by nature, he became almost unbearable after the accident. The boys suffered his abusive explosions of temper and so did his white-haired wife Hattie, who had to wait on him day and night. The entire family attributed most of their misery to the mine men who were now standing just twenty feet away from the brothers in the Palace. Ike, the oldest, wasn't about to pass up the opportunity to vent his anger on the pair.

'What kind of a real man would drink girlie slop like that!' He turned to his brothers, his voice loud enough to be heard throughout the big room.

'That's about what I'd expect from a pair of dirt diggers,' Elwood chimed in, glaring down the bar. 'They'd probably choke on a real whiskey.' He followed up with a forced laugh.

Rolo and Edward turned, facing the brothers. They'd seen the four when they came in, choosing to ignore them on purpose. 'We're not bothering anyone in here, including you. Why don't you try acting like civilized men instead of backwoods fools?' Mackenzie answered back, as Chambers tugged at his sleeve, shaking his head to warn him not to go any further.

'Civilized men?' Ike parroted, straightening up. 'Why would we want to act like you two? You send men down into the ground then bring them up dead in ore carts from breathing poisoned air. Is that what you two call civilized? I'd call that pure murder. You two ought to be hung for it!'

'Don't waste any more time talking to them.' Chambers leaned close, whispering to his partner. 'It's only going to lead to trouble we don't need. Come on. Drink up and let's leave.'

Mackenzie nodded but couldn't let

6

Ike get in the last word in front of everyone listening. 'We offered you and your family a fair price for your place and you refused to sell and make some real money for once. Why complain now because your neighbours did? You had your chance and didn't have enough brains to take it.'

'Who you callin' stupid?' Ike exploded, stepping away from the bar, his hand going down, gripping the pistol, pulling it up. 'Take it back or I'll spill your guts all over this floor!'

Rolo lifted both hands, palms up. 'I'm not armed. Don't do something you'll get yourself hung for. There's twenty people in here who'll swear to it at a trial.'

Ike's beady eyes darted around the room and back to Mackenzie. That's when he saw the bartender straightening up from behind the counter with a 12 gauge shotgun, levelling the ugly scattergun on him.

'Don't pull that six gun, or I'll fill you up with buckshot, Ike. You and your

7

brothers go on and get out of here. Don't come back until you can control yourselves. I'm not going to have a killing in here over you, your brothers, or anyone else. Move it!'

Ike eyed the barkeep with the same rage he had Mackenzie. Virgil grabbed him by the shoulder. 'Come on, Ike. Let's go. It ain't worth gettin' killed over. Our time will come on these two.'

The brothers herded Ike toward the front door as customers parted, giving them a clear exit, but not before Ike shouted one last threat.

'I'll be remembering you pulled that scattergun on me. Don't think I won't!'

As the room settled down and talk resumed again, the barman turned to Rolo.

'Don't turn your back on him or his brothers. Ike's half crazy. Always has been. He'll try to get even with you. You better know that. The whole bunch of them up there in that broken-down ranch are all the same. Vernal, their father, is the worst of the bunch because he encourages the boys to always pick a fight with anyone for any reason.'

'I think I'll have a second brandy.' Rolo let out a long sigh of relief, leaning back on the bar. 'That's about as close as I want to come to being shot.'

Hattie Goss, Vernal's wife, lit the lantern over the dinner table as her sons carried Vernal in from the front porch, carefully lowering him into his chair at the head of the table. The four boys glanced at each other trying to decide if they should tell their father what happened in town at the Grand Palace. Hattie brought over a large kettle of soup, filled with a few thin scraps of meat. She ladled out Vernal's portion first; he glared down at the meagre provender, then up at her, scowling in displeasure.

'Is this all the meat you can put in here? There's hardly enough to feed a man!'

'It's all we have, Vernal. If the boys can kill a buck we could have some venison. Right now we don't have much else.' She avoided his cold stare.

'There's no bucks to kill around here any more,' Emmett growled. 'With them dynamite blasts going off all the time they ran all the deer outta here.'

'Yeah, them mine men have wrecked everything,' Elwood spoke up. 'They even tried to buffalo Ike, in town this afternoon.'

The boys glanced at each other fearing Elwood's big mouth would get them all in trouble but it was too late. They had good reason to worry as Vernal turned to Ike with a withering stare.

'What's your brother talking about, Ike? Who tried to buffalo you? I want to hear it all.'

'They pulled a shotgun on me — or it wouldn't have happened like it did.' He looked up at Elwood, avoiding his father's icy stare.

'I said who pulled a shotgun on you? What are you talking about? Give me a name!' Vernal's voice rose to a vicious snarl.

Ike slowly explained what happened at the Grand Palace, and the bartender's role in it. By the time he finished, Vernal's lips were quivering in rage as beads of sweat broke out on his wrinkled forehead.

'You let them fools do that to you? Where were the rest of you boys?' He looked around the table. 'Why didn't you back your brother up, like I always taught you?'

'We couldn't do nothin', Paw. With that scattergun on Ike, the barman would have cut him to pieces,' Elwood tried to explain.

Vernal slumped back in his chair closing his eyes for a moment, his jaw set tight in rage. He'd had about all he could take because of the mine men since they'd come to Peralta, and what they'd done buying up everything around him. What happened to Ike was the last straw. No one could push around the Goss family without paying a price. Chambers and Mackenzie were the ones who would pay it now.

11

A week had passed since the altercation at the Grand Palace. Rolo and his partner sat in their office, working at separate desks. Rolo took a break, turning to Edward.

'Don't you think it's time Peralta had some kind of law?'

Chambers looked up from the map he was studying. 'Well, now that the town is starting to really grow, that might be something for folks around here to think about. Up until now they settled things on their own.'

'Yes, like the Goss brothers. Pull a gun and pull the trigger. I think it's time those days came to an end. We've got a solid business going here and more people and money will want to come in. They won't if it gets around that this is a wide open, lawless town.'

Chambers thought a moment before answering. 'Having a full-time lawman might be something folks could consider, but I also know a lot of people living outside town might not be that eager for it. They still live by the law of the land.'

Rolo rested his chin on his hand, thinking over the exchange. 'That could be, but I still say Peralta is ready for it. Why don't we see if we can generate some interest by talking to other businessmen? Let's see if they're willing to contribute money each month to pay a decent sheriff's wages.'

Edward smiled at his partner's enthusiasm. Rolo always thought people had a streak of decency in them, no matter how much they seemed the opposite. He wondered if the face-off in the Grand Palace had anything to do with Rolo's sudden suggestion to bring in a star man. His partner was a decent, hard-working man who always thought principles were important. That's one reason he joined him in this business venture of theirs. If he wanted to try for law in Peralta, then he was on board to help him.

'I guess we can contribute some

13

money if you want. Others might join us too. After all, we are making good money with the mining except for having to freight the ore all the way down to Marysville, for crushing and smelting. The price of mercury down there doesn't help either, but right now we have no other choice. It's a four-day round trip no matter how we do it. And it might be a good idea to have some protection when John Standard is hauling silver bars and money back up here too. I've also been thinking we're going to have to work out a better plan to sell our silver in Nevada. The silver mining around Carson City is supposed to be getting big and we can save money if we find a buyer there.'

'I've thought about John handling all those bars and money too. I know it's dangerous, but John is certainly not a man to be pushed around by anyone. He's got a solid reputation, that's for sure. Having some law here also helps that idea.'

'Have you ever considered hiring a

guard to ride with him when he goes down to Marysville? As this town grows, not everyone coming here is going to be an angel. The talk of big money always seems to bring trouble in with it.'

'Let's talk to John about it when he gets back. I'd like to know what he thinks. He's the one who has to carry all the bullion and cash.'

* * *

John Standard sat atop the big freight wagon pulled by four strong horses, urging them up the steep slope leaving Marysville. It was a long, slow climb back to Peralta, one he'd made several times before. At fifty-one years old he had a solid reputation as a deft hand when it came to horses and freighting. In his younger years he'd driven stage coaches in southern Colorado, where he garnered the name 'Shotgun John' for the deadly double barrel he always carried up in the coach boot. Rumour had it he'd used the scattergun on more than one occasion and never been robbed of a single nickel. He was a quiet man who never talked about those early years. He let his reputation do the talking for him. He was hauling timber for shoring up the mines when he met Chambers and Mackenzie, who hired him away from his employer. He also knew all too well that the silver ingots and money he was instructed to bring back each trip were goods to be protected at all costs. His trusty double barrel was still kept rolled up in a blanket under his seat, but he'd never had any occasion to use it. At his age he knew he wasn't as fast or agile as he was at twenty-five or thirty. Knowing it was there was comforting. He secretly hoped he'd never have to use it again. That's one of the reasons why on this return trip he'd decided to leave Marysville as the long shadows of evening spread their fingers across the rolling flatlands instead of daylight. The road was empty now and cooling

16

nighttime temperatures were easier on the horses. He liked driving under a sky full of diamond-bright stars with a cool breeze on his cheeks. John pulled his jacket collar up higher, urging the horses ahead, working his fingers deeper into his gloves. He'd always thought it odd that nighttime hours passed faster than the same length of time during the day. From one to five during daylight hours always seemed to be a slow crawl but at night it flew by. This night was no different as the miles steadily slipped away behind the wagon, climbing higher as the horses blew, straining at the traces. The peaceful quietness was comforting as the big freighter rattled on.

Dawn was just a crimson slash along the eastern horizon when the freight wagon topped another high ridge. John pulled the horses to a stop giving them a much-needed breather. He stood stretching out some of the kinks, arms above his shoulders, when suddenly a rough voice rang out from murky shadows alongside the trail.

'You just keep them arms right up there over yer head, if you know what's good fer you. And don't try for that scattergun under the seat, neither!'

John could barely make out the shadows of four riders emerging from tall brush toward the wagon. He'd never been held up freighting for the mine men and he didn't want to start now. But four pistols levelled on him was the worst kind of odds to go up against. He knew if he was going to act it had be fast, right now, or not at all. He chose now. Suddenly dropping to his knees he dove for the shotgun, trying to unravel it from the blanket as six guns exploded and bullets tore into him, their flashes lighting up the dawn sky. He fell forward on to the floorboards moaning in pain, unable to move yet still semi-conscious.

'Git up there and open that cash box!' Ike shouted to Virgil. 'Emmett, you get in back and get some of them silver bars too. Hurry, we ain't got all night!'

'The box is bolted to the floor!' Virgil yelled, rolling Standard out of the way.

'Then shoot the lock off, you idiot. Do I have to tell you everything?'

'These silver bars are way too heavy for us to carry very many.' Emmett dumped several at the back of the wagon.

'Then just git enough to fill our saddle-bags, and let's git outa here,' Ike ordered.

Virgil's six gun thundered, shattering the hasp lock on the box. Reaching inside he drew out two heavy canvas sacks of gold and silver coins. 'I got it, Ike!'

'Pick up those silver bars too!' Ike shouted.

Through a staggering wall of pain John heard the shouts and orders. He heard the names too, if he could just live long enough to tell someone. Next came the pounding hooves of horses running fast, fading away into an awakening sky. John tried to catch his breath even though he could not rise from the floorboards. Slowly his left hand crawled up to the foot board. He felt the reins in his hand. Gripping them with what little strength he could summon, he slapped them down just once before collapsing on the floor.

'Git up — to town.' He rolled over on his back. The last thing he saw was those icy bright stars silently staring down on him.

A cold drizzle that started just before sunrise made the wagon road slick and muddy. The big freighter moved along at a slow pace without a driver to control the horses. But the animals knew the way back to town and kept plodding ahead mile after mile, until late that afternoon when the irregular shapes of buildings loomed up ahead through surrounding timber. The team picked up their pace. Several men crossing the street looked up as the wagon came into the far end of town, until one turned to his pals, stopping them.

'Ain't that John Standard's wagon?

But where's he at? There's no one up in the seat.'

The trio ran to the wagon, pulling the horses to a halt, while one man climbed up. 'Good God, it's John, and it looks like he's been shot. Someone get some help!'

People on the street heard the shout and came running as one bystander ran for the doctor's office. Chambers and Mackenzie heard the commotion, going to their office window and looking out to see their wagon with a crowd of people gathering. 'Something's happened. Let's get out there.' Chambers headed for the door with Rolo right on his heels.

Reaching the wagon, people were already lifting Standard out, laying him on the ground. One look at his cold, grey, lined face and bloody bullet holes in his jacket made it clear a doctor couldn't help the old man. That he was even still alive was a miracle of will from the tough old whip man. Rolo knelt next to him, carefully wiping blood from his white whiskered mouth.

'John, who did this — can you tell me? Try, John. Please try.'

Rolo leaned closer hoping to hear a whisper, but all he heard was a death rattle breath gasping for air. Unable to answer, John looked up with desperation in his eyes. Very slowly he half raised one hand uncoiling four gnarled, bloody fingers. He lifted it higher, nearly touching Rolo's face, before collapsing back down and closing his eyes.

'What's he trying to say?' Rolo looked up to Chambers, in desperation.

'I don't know.' Edward shook his head. 'It must mean something important. He managed to keep himself alive long enough to get back here and tell us.'

The doctor came running down the street, bag in hand, pushing his way through the crowd, kneeling at John's side.

'You've got to help him, doc,' Mackenzie pleaded. 'Do something, anything to save him.'

The doctor leaned lower, carefully placing his finger on Standard's jugular vein. After a moment he looked back at Rolo. 'The only thing I can do for your friend is get the undertaker over here. I'm sorry, Rolo, he's gone.'

Rolo's head dropped as his hand grabbed John's shoulder, and tears filled his eyes. When he'd composed himself enough to speak again he looked up at Chambers.

'I think we need that law we've been talking about now more than ever. Don't you, Edward?'

Chambers slowly nodded without speaking. Robbery and cold-blooded murder had come to Peralta. Both men knew town would never be the same because of it.

2

Benjamin Dickson was a most unusual lawman by any measure. Some said, always behind his back, he wasn't a real lawman at all, only using an old marshal's badge he carried to justify his depredations against those who went outside his brand of law. There was no disputing he was a rare breed whose reputation was so well known that he literally hired himself and his gun out as sheriff, deputy or marshal, but not for the paltry sum of twenty dollars a month, what most town sheriffs were being paid. His monthly fee to clean out any lawless town was four hundred dollars per man, take it or leave it. Most took it. Towns desperate for law, businessmen who wanted certain people eliminated, cattle interests tired of having beef rustled and missing, all paid up — and gladly. Dickson's tenure in any town rarely lasted more than one or two months after he'd cleaned out the problem and buried men on Boot Hill in a cheap pine box. At forty-one, an even six feet tall, athletically fit, he was at the top of his game. He could cold track men for days on end in wild country never lighting a fire, eating little until running them down, or force a showdown right on the main street in front of crowds. Ben Dickson didn't care either way. The sooner he took care of business, the sooner he got paid and was on to his next assignment. He always had rich customers waiting in line.

Dickson was not a man to kid himself either. He knew time and age would eventually slow him down and take its toll on reflexes and gun speed. He had to make all the big money he could, and make it over the next ten years. After that he'd hang up his weapons and move someplace where no one knew his name or fame. That was the fate of every gunman sooner or later, on either side of the law. Those that did not ended up lying in the street, or barroom floor, or on lonely trails dying in their own blood. He'd made up his mind when he chose this way of life he would never be one of them.

Dickson's specialty was a custom-made Colt .45 caliber six gun trigger honed for a light fast pull. It gave him that split-second edge when facing trouble. He backed that up with a wicked sawed-off 12 gauge shotgun. Those eighteen-inch twin barrels of death aimed at anyone had an instant effect. The man facing them either threw up his hands or was cut nearly in two by a double load of lead buckshot belt-buckle high. There was never any 'grey' area about those he deemed guilty. They were outside Dickson's Law, and had to pay for it one way or the other. Dickson always preferred to settle any matter with guns. Trials, lawyers and juries took too much time and sometimes made the wrong decisions because of oily haired, fast talking, slick lawyers. His brand of justice was fast and final.

Once, and only once, he'd nearly been killed early in his career by an ambush in Indian Territory, chasing a band of renegade Apaches. In the shootout that followed his right leg was so badly shot up it had to be amputated below the knee. Before he made it back to a doctor, he killed all three red men. The result was that he had a hard-wood leg from the knee down and walked with a slightly pronounced gait. As far as handling weapons and shooting accurately, it had no effect whatsoever. That was determined by an iron will and gun practice. He had plenty of both.

Dickson sat propped up in a chair on the front porch of the Double Hot Hotel, in Rincon Valley, Arizona, when a young boy came running down the boardwalk stopping to stare up at the feared lawman.

'Mr Stevens down at the telegraph office told me to get this to you real quick, sir. Here it is.' He handed over a note, wide-eyed in awe.

Dickson reached into his vest pocket, handing the lad two bits for his trouble.

'Jeeze, thanks Mr Dickson. I can buy me a whole lot of penny candy with this!'

As the pint-sized messenger ran back down the walkway, Dickson unfolded the paper and began to read.

Mr Benjamin Dickson
Rincon, Arizona
Dear Sir,
We are in need of your special services here in Peralta, Colorado. Your usual fee will be paid in advance upon your arrival. If you are interested in this offer please let us know at your earliest convenience. We look forward to hearing from you.
I remain,
Rolo Mackenzie.

Dickson eased to his feet, stretching out the kinks for a moment. The summer sun was coming and no place was hotter than Arizona. Colorado would be cooler. He liked the thought of it. The job and timing were a perfect fit. It was a long ride but the one hundred dollar retainer would make that easier. If there was either state or federal 'paper' on whoever Mr Mackenzie wanted taken care of, he'd pocket that money too. He wired his acceptance down at the telegraph office, then stopped by the livery stable to have his horse and a packer prepared for the trail. Back at the hotel, he paid up his bill.

'You look like a man about to leave town, Mr Dickson,' the counterman quipped, a thin smile playing across his face.

'Yes, but hold my room for me as usual. I shouldn't be gone too long. And keep the cleaning lady out of there too. I want no one in my room while I'm gone. You understand?'

'I do, sir. Have a good trip.'

'I intend to.'

* ★ ★

Three weeks later Ben Dickson rode down Main Street in Peralta, to the stares of some on the boardwalk. It only took one look to see this new stranger was no knock-about cowboy. Not with his fine horse, big packer and expensive trail clothes. He rode slowly down the street reading each business sign until he came to the 'Chambers & Mackenzie Mining Company'. Reining in, he eased out of the saddle, tying off his horse and packer. Stepping up on the boardwalk, he pushed through the front door into the office. Rolo was first to turn from his desk. Getting to his feet he came to the counter, studying the tall man in expensive clothes.

'I'll bet you're Ben Dickson, aren't you?'

'Yes, I am. And how did you come to that?'

'Because you're exactly what I thought you'd look like.' He extended his hand over the counter top with a small smile, introducing himself.

Chambers quickly crossed the room,

shaking hands before inviting Dickson into the office and offering him a chair.

'Care for a cup of hot coffee, Mr Dickson?' Edward offered.

'After my long ride, don't mind if I do. Then I want to get down to business about whatever problem you're having here in Peralta. The sooner I know what and who that is, the sooner I can resolve it for you. I want both of you to tell me everything you know or think you know. Don't leave out any detail, no matter how small you believe it might be. Anything you tell me can be important.'

He shucked off his heavy trail coat as Rolo and Edward shot knowing glances at each other. Already they knew this was a man who meant business. Anyone of his stature who spoke with authority and carrying a big pearl-handled Colt pistol to back it up, had to be exactly what they'd hoped for.

'I can tell you straight off we have a pretty good idea who we think robbed our freight wagon and killed the driver,'

Rolo was quick to volunteer.

'If you're that sure, why haven't you done something about it?'

'Because there is no law here in Peralta. And we're not much good at taking it into our own hands. That's why we need a man with your expertize.'

'I see.' He nodded. 'You have a name for me?'

'Yes. There's a backwoods family that lives outside of town named Goss. The old man, Vernal, has four grown sons. They're about as wild as the place they live in. They've made threats before but we never thought it was that serious. You know, just tough talk. There's been a lot of bad blood over an offer we made to buy their property to expand our mining. The old man refused it. He leads his boys around and they do whatever he tells them to. He's a cripple and the real trouble in the family. He spreads his misery around to all the boys and they don't dare question him.'

Vernal Goss sat at the kitchen table ordering his wife Hattie and the boys to sit down around him as she nervously twisted her fingers, fearing what tirade he'd come up with next. He looked from Ike to Virgil first then Elwood and Emmett, with the same squinty-eyed stare. 'Did you bury them silver bars like I told ya to?'

'We sure did, Paw. Just like you said. We buried them above the spring in that rocky ground behind the house. We even put a mule shoe between two flat rocks pointing right at the spot so Elwood and Emmett can find them if we're not around when you want them.'

'All right then. I'm glad to see you two had enough brains to use your heads for once. Now listen to me and listen real good. We can't go around flashin' any of that money from the hold-up, or try to sell those silver bars anyplace around here. It's too risky. Someone would sure take notice that all of a sudden us poor folks came into big money. You might have to take the buckboard and go all the way down to Marysville, or head over the mountain to Fool's Gold, to sell 'em off. For what little food we buy in town, you can use some of the money but not too much. Don't never go in there with a pocket full of cash. We gotta be careful and smart about how we use it.'

'I heard someone in town say the wagon driver died right there on the street,' Ike added. 'I never figured that old bird would ever make it that far after the holes we put in him.'

'And they said he never told who took him down, either. We got lucky on that one.' Virgil nodded, looking around the table for agreement.

'Killin' can bring trouble, but if the driver was fool enough to go for a boot gun, then you've got no choice. Next time remember that. If you can get the cash box without killin', do it. If you can't, do what you have to. We're gonna break these mine men until they don't have two bits left to their stinkin' name, and they pack up and go someplace else to wreck the country. I've had a belly full of 'em around here!'

★ ★ ★

Dickson left the mine office with the news Peralta had no hotel, only a boarding house one block over from Main Street, surrounded by family homes. When he rode up to the two-storey building he wasn't impressed. He stood for a moment taking it all in. Paint peeled off the old clapboard siding and dusty curtains hung on windows. He steeled himself; he wasn't going to have the niceties of the Double Hot Hotel. It was all the more reason to get to the bottom of the freight wagon robbery and killing as fast as possible and move on. At least Rolo and Chambers had given him a good start about the Goss family. He tied off the horses, unbuckling two bags and heading for the front door.

'I serve a light breakfast, no lunch

but a good size dinner.' Birdie Lee, the owner of the house was quick to lay down house rules. Lee was a small, wiry-looking woman in her late forties with a mean mouth that looked like she could bite a double eagle in half. 'I don't allow no liquor in the rooms, and no women snuck in here after hours either. If I find any of that going on you're gone right then.'

Dickson eyed her coolly. 'How much for a room in this princely palace?'

'It's three dollars a night, paid in advance. I don't take no credit or trade. Even though you don't look much like you'd do either.' She'd already sized up his clothes, big hat and fancy hand-made knee-high boots. 'You here in Peralta on business?' She took the chance she might draw him out for an answer.

'Yes — personal business. For three dollars a night it stays that way — personal. Here's twenty dollars for the rest of the week, and I want someone to knock on my door half an hour before meals are served. Here's an extra four dollars to cover that before you ask.' He pushed the bills over the counter, as she eyed his wallet, thick with more bills.

For once Birdie was caught speechless. When she recovered seconds later she said she'd have someone notify him about the meals. 'You're the first door at the top of the stairs on the right, room five.' She pushed the key across the counter.

'Does anyone else have a key to my room?' Dickson questioned. 'Yes, I do. I have to in case you leave or get locked out.'

'Give me that key. I want no one having access to my room whether I'm in it or not. You'll get both keys back when I leave. You don't have to worry about that. You have a handyman or some kind of help around here?'

'I have a young kid who run errands for me and helps out.'

'Tell him I want my horses taken down to the livery stable to get a good feed on oats and a rest. Here's another five to take care of that.'

Dickson started up the stairs as Birdie watched him go. He's an odd one, she thought. But at least he was willing to pay for everything he wanted. She wondered what would possibly bring a man like that to Peralta. He seemed so out of place here.

* * *

A knock on the door next morning woke Dickson. He rolled over looking at the clock on the dresser; 6:45 am. A muffled voice on the other side announced, 'Breakfast in thirty minutes, Mr Dickson.'

Dickson didn't answer. Sitting up on the edge of the bed he reached over to the nightstand, retrieving his hardwood lower leg. Slipping a sock on his stump he pulled the heavy leather collar attached to it up over his knee and began lacing up the leather thongs snug around his leg. Standing, he tested the fit before slipping into boots, fresh shirt and pants. He stood before the floor mirror taking several steps toward it. Satisfied his gait looked natural enough he went to the wash basin on the dresser, cleaning his face, combing long, dark hair, and lastly trimming his moustache.

Retrieving a leather case, he opened the locks, lifting out the custom-made Colt .45. Buckling up his belt, he slid the six-gun into its holster. The weight of it always felt good against his leg. He never felt whole without it. After shucking into a coat and pulling on his wide-brimmed hat, Dickson exited the room, locking the door behind him and starting downstairs.

Entering the dining room, Dickson noticed half a dozen people already seated at the table passing food trays. All eyes turned to him when he came into the room, especially Birdie Lee.

'I trust you enjoyed a good night's sleep?' Birdie warily tried to start off the conversation on a positive note.

'It was passable,' he answered, reaching for a large platter stacked with bacon and eggs. 'Pass the coffee pot, would you? Do you know what time the livery stable opens?'

'I think Horace opens at eight o'clock, sir,' a young man at the far end of the table answered, obviously the breakfast announcer and handyman at the house. An elderly woman sat quietly next to Birdie. Dickson took her for a permanent resident or possibly a relative. Two middle-aged men dressed in suits ate at the middle of the table, announcing they were in Peralta to sell dry goods and tack equipment. One studied Dickson a moment before posing a question.

'And what is your trade, Mr Dickson?'

'I'm a hunter.'

'Ah, I love hunting. When I was a boy back in Ohio, I used to chase those cottontail rabbits round and round. Making a living at it must be exciting up here in mountain country.'

'It can be, especially if they fire back.'

An attractive woman in her early thirties with long auburn hair sat on the opposite side of the table without speaking. Birdie noticed Dickson glancing at her. She decided it might be another opening.

'Mrs June is travelling all the way to California, to meet her husband. She's staying here for a short rest from rough stage travel. Those coaches are not the most comfortable things after weeks of getting jostled around in one. Will you be back for dinner tonight Mr Dickson, too?'

'I expect to be.' He finished a quick breakfast, getting to his feet. 'Good day, madam.'

At the livery stable Dickson saddled his horse, sliding the sawed-off shotgun into a specially made scabbard. Rolo had drawn him a rough map showing how to reach the Goss ranch. He studied it a moment before saddling up and starting out of town. The ride took just over an hour, passing several mining locations with men working around them, until reaching a remote canyon beyond all the activity. Dickson reined to a stop, studying the scene. On the opposite side hill surrounded by scattered timber sat the dishevelled ranch. Dickson urged his horse closer until seeing Vernal Goss, sitting on the front porch with a blanket over his knees and a shotgun in his lap. The tall man rode right up to the rickety porch in his usual confrontational manner without a hail as the two iron-willed men stared at each other, until Vernal spoke.

'If you've rode all the way out here to make me another offer to sell my place, turn that nag around and go back and tell those two crooks I ain't sellin'!'

Dickson pulled his horse around so the badge on his lapel could be easily seen.

'I'm not here to make you any offers for anything. This is official business. I'm here to talk to those boys of yours and get some answers. Get them out here.'

Vernal stiffened at the tone of his voice. No one talked to him like that and got away with it, not even some fancy-dressed stranger with a tin star pinned on him. His short temper began to rise as his arthritic hands gripped the shotgun tighter, slowly sliding the barrels around toward Dickson, with a silent threat.

'Who in hell do you think you are to come ridin' in here on my place and start barking orders? This is Goss ground you're on. I could take you out of the saddle with one barrel, if I had a mind to!'

'No you won't. Because before you ever got that stove pipe up, you'd be dead. You're too old and slow to out-pull me and you know it. Now where's those boys of yours? Get them out here or I'll go in and get them myself.'

'You try that and I'll cut you down before you make two steps. That tin badge of yours don't mean nothin' out here. I know who sent you. Those two mine men back in town. I'll tell you just once my boys ain't here and you better believe it. You got no reason to be out here except if someone was paying you, and I know who that has to be.'

'I'm a US Marshal. My badge is good anywhere I go. That includes right here. You better not be lying to me about your sons. If you are I'll take you in too.'

Vernal hesitated. He wasn't quite sure what to do next. For the first time in years he'd run up against someone he couldn't buffalo and who was packing a tin star to boot. He took in a deep breath, trying to decide how to answer without backing down.

'I said they ain't here and that's the truth of it.'

'Where are they then?'

'I don't know. Out huntin' some-place.'

'Where?'

'I said I don't know. It could be anyplace. We need meat.'

Dickson eyed the old man, trying to

44

decide if he was lying or not.

'When they get back I'm coming out here again. Understand? And they better be ready to start answering some questions, or I'll swear out warrants against all of you. You tell them that and you make it stick. I'll see you real soon again.'

Dickson pulled his horse around, starting away as Vernal watched him go. The old man's hands shook uncontrollably from tremors plus the nervous tension of being confronted so roughly. If there was one thing Dickson's visit made clear it was that he had to be killed and fast. Vernal knew Dickson was working on the wagon hold-up and murder of John Standard. That could get them all hung. The sooner the boys got back, the sooner he'd come up with a plan to see to it Ben Dickson never made a second ride back to his ranch.

Ike, Virgil, Emmett and Elwood returned the next day with good news. They'd sold off the silver bars, but they barely had time to rejoice over it when

Vernal told them about yesterday's visitor.

'He's gotta be killed, and I mean right now,' Vernal demanded. 'I don't want to hafta see you boys dangling from the end of a rope, and neither does your mother!'

His sudden announcement brought the conversation to an immediate stop. Ike looked around the table at his brothers, then back to his father. 'Paw, I ain't so sure killin' a lawman is a good idea. Besides, he don't know nothin'. Let 'em come back. We ain't gonna tell him anything anyway.'

'Yeah, Paw,' Virgil added. 'Why get in any deeper than we already are? No one knows we held up the freight wagon. But if we kill this lawman, they'll just send others after him. I think Ike is right.'

'You listen to me, you idiots.' Vernal Goss pounded the table, eyes widening in anger. 'Dickson is already pretty certain you four took that wagon. Any little slip-up you make he'll use as an excuse to take you in. We can't take no chance like that. The longer he's on the loose poking around, the more chance he might turn up something. If I could get up out of this chair, I'd do it my own self, but I can't. He said he'd be back in a day or two. You gotta see to it he never does come back. He must be stayin' in town and there's only one boarding house, Birdie Lee's. Night-time is the best time to find him and do what you have to. He's got to move around to go eat or maybe to a saloon or over to the livery stable. He's easy to spot. He's about six foot tall, wears a big-brimmed hat, fancy clothes and some sort of high-topped lace-up boots. He's probably with them mine men so look for him there too. He's also got a fancy six gun with pearl handles on it. There ain't nobody else in Peralta looks like that. You four go in there and watch where he goes, then do your job. That's how we solve this lawman problem real fast!'

3

When Dickson got back into town after confronting Vernal, he stopped by the mine office just as Rolo and Edward were closing up for lunch. Rolo unlocked the door inviting Dickson back inside, anxious to hear what happened at the Goss ranch.

'Did you see the brothers?' Mackenzie quickly questioned.

'No, just the old man. He's enough trouble on his own. Twisted up like he is makes him even more mean and dangerous. He likes to wave a shotgun around too. He's lucky I didn't have paper on his boys. I would have had to disarm him — with my own shotgun. That might happen sooner or later before all this is over.'

'Where are his sons at?' Chambers asked.

'He says they're in some town called

Fool's Gold. Is there such a place, or was that just a lie?'

'Yes there is. It's over the mountains, several days' ride from here. They do a good deal of both hard rock gold and silver mining. Like us they have to haul their ore all the way down to Marysville for smelting. I don't know why his boys would be going over there. None of them ever worked a day for anyone, and especially not back-breaking mine work,' Rolo wondered.

'Maybe they didn't go there at all? Maybe it's all just a lie,' Chambers suggested.

'Either way I told the old man I'd be back to question those four of them and that's exactly what I mean to do. I'll do it one at a time away from each other. If they try lying, I'll find out quick enough.'

'We're going out to eat tonight at the Grand Palace. Would you care to join us so we can talk about this some more?' Mackenzie invited.

'That might be a change of pace from

Birdie's boarding house. What time are you eating?'

'Say, about six thirty?'

'All right. I'll meet you there. I've got a few things I want to buy before the stores close and that'll give me plenty of time. See you then.'

Dickson exited the office, starting up the street as the mine men went to the window watching him go.

'Can you imagine him riding right up to Goss and confronting him like that?' Rolo shook his head in amazement.

'Yes, I can. He's that kind of a man. I'd say he's lived his life doing the very same thing in other places to dangerous men. He's one of a kind for sure. Looks like we hired the right man for the job. Neither Vernal or his boys are going to be pushed very far before they push back. Dickson's heading for a showdown one way or the other. They're like rattlesnakes in a boot. Shake it a little and it strikes back. It's just a matter of time before something happens — and I don't think much time at that.'

That evening after the sun went down, Ike pulled his horse to a stop in an alley one block behind Main Street, followed by his brothers. He had the plan his father had told him to follow to find and kill Ben Dickson. The old man said it was best done after dark when no one could see who did the shooting. Ike went over those orders again for the tenth time, repeating it to himself at a whisper so he wouldn't get it wrong. Gathering his brothers around as the misty shadows of evening descended on Peralta, and kerosene lamps blinked on all over town, he repeated them now.

'Virgil, Paw said you're supposed to take one side of Main Street and watch fer Dickson. Remember he's about six foot tall and carries a big, pearl handled revolver and wears some kind of funny knee-high lace-up boots and fancy clothes. Elwood, do the same on the other side of the street. Most stores are closin' by now so look in saloons, gambling houses or maybe restaurants. Emmett and me are goin' over to Birdie

Lee's boarding house. Paw thinks he has to be stayin' there. If you find him don't try to kill him by yourself. Meet back here in one hour and we'll all gang up on 'em at the same time. Let's git to it.'

Virgil and his brother went down a narrow alley to Main Street. Already the growing darkness made the forms of the men and women passing by into shadowy silhouettes. Virgil crossed the street, leaning up against a store front. He could just make out Elwood across from him. Both brothers watched people passing by for several minutes before growing restless, moving down the street and stopping to look in those few places still open. At the Gambler's Den faro house, Virgil stepped inside. Already the smoky room was beginning to fill up with evening gamblers of every description and dress and the noise of excited gambling men. Not one came close to matching the description Vernal had given him. He stepped back outside, continuing up the street.

Elwood saw his brother disappear into the faro room, prompting him to start up his side of the street. At the door leading into Tong Sing's Chinese restaurant, he stopped, trying to stare inside at dark figures sitting at tables and moving across the narrow, cramped room. He could just make out Sing's tiny wife bringing steaming hot dishes to tables as the delicious aroma of strange food wafted outside into his face. He pulled the back of his hand across his drooling mouth before stopping himself, remembering he had a job to do. No one inside seemed to fit the description he had of Dickson. Turning away, he continued up the boardwalk passing dark storefronts, already closed for the evening.

Ike and Emmett trudged the three blocks to Birdie Lee's boarding house. Behind curtained windows, the soft glow of kerosene lamps lit the night as the pair came to a stop in front of the building. 'We can't see nothin' from here,' Ike whispered. 'Let's git up closer and peek through them windows.'

Emmett nodded without answering. They pushed through a squeaky gate, tip-toeing up to the first window. Ike pressed his whiskery face against the glass, trying to make out the figures sitting around a table inside.

'Can you see anything?' Elwood asked.

'Unh-unh. Let's try another window,' he grunted.

Starting for the living room window, Emmett suddenly tripped on shrubbery, falling flat on his face with a loud grunt. As Ike leaned down to help him up, the front door suddenly opened and a tall man wearing a wide-brimmed hat stepped out, closing it behind him and starting down the steps. Ike flattened himself next to his brother, only yards away in the dark. As the man passed they squinted up, seeing the reflection of starlight off a pearl-handled revolver before he pushed through the squeaky gate, starting towards town. The pair lay there, still not daring to breathe as Ike's hand reached up gripping Elwood's shoulder and digging in deep. When footsteps faded away, Ike whispered in his brother's ear, 'That's him — it's gotta be!'

Dickson walked steadily toward Main Street in his usual off-step gait. Halfway there he until suddenly spun on his good leg, pulling his six-gun, peering hard into the dark behind him. Ike and Emmett immediately sunk to the ground. Dickson thought he'd heard a noise that shouldn't be there. For several seconds longer he did not move, listening, straining to see something, anything, only to be met by complete silence. Very slowly Dickson slid the big Colt back in its holster, taking one more long look back before starting again for his dinner engagement. Ike and Elwood stayed flat on the ground with their faces in the dirt, waiting for the tall man to fade away before pulling themselves back to their feet.

'You big dumbbell,' Ike threatened. 'Be quiet. You almost got us both shot!'

Reaching the lights of Main Street,

Ben Dickson strode up the boardwalk toward the Grand Palace, passing mostly men out for the evening. Approaching the front door, his attention was drawn to a weedy-looking man leaning up against the building near the entry. The tall, skinny stranger wore a tattered hat and threadbare clothes. His unkempt, whiskered beard largely hid his face except for a pair of small, beady eyes. As Dickson passed he also saw the butt of a six-gun sticking up in the man's pants top under a dirty long overcoat. Their eyes met for just an instant. It was a cold, dead stare as Dickson stepped past him, going into the big room.

Passing through the busy bar, Dickson entered the dining room. Rolo and Edward were already at their table as Rolo waved him over. 'You're right on time,' he noted, as Dickson sat down.

'I try to be. I've always lived pretty much by the clock,' Dickson answered.

'We haven't ordered yet, but I can recommend the steak. It's good grass-fed beef from down around Marysville.'

'Steak it is then. And a good bottle of whiskey would also sit well on the stomach. While we're waiting for dinner, tell me more about this Goss family.' He eased into a chair.

An unopened bottle of whiskey plus three glasses were brought to the table by their waiter, a small man with a neatly-trimmed beard and moustache, met by curly sideburns around his face. Dickson unsealed the top, pouring three stubby glasses full to the brim. 'Salute,' he toasted. 'Here's to quick success in our venture.'

Dickson sipped at the amber coloured liquid while the mine men filled him in on what else they knew about Vernal Goss and his sons, plus their reputation as loners even to people here in town. They also brought up the verbal battles and threats they'd had with the old man when they made him offers to buy his property. Dickson listened thoughtfully for several minutes before posing a question.

'Has there been any other robberies

or hold-ups here before you two had your wagon man robbed and killed?'

'Only a few small thefts like businesses broken into at night, food or supplies taken. Most people thought it was just drifters passing through or miners down on their luck. There wasn't any reason to expect anyone in town would do something like that. John's murder is the first serious thing Peralta has ever had happen. We've had some scrapes, threats and fist fights, but nothing like what happened to John. Peralta has never even had a sheriff. That's why we contacted you. His murder has to be settled and those that did it brought to justice, or the word gets out you can do anything you want up here and get away with it. That kind of wanton brutality and disrespect for human life cannot be tolerated. This town has to grow and have a reputation that grows with it,' Chambers said, leaning forward for emphasis.

Outside in the night, Virgil moved from the front window facing the bar to a second one into the dining room. He pressed close against the glass, looking until he saw Mackenzie and Chambers engaged in conversation with a man whose back was to him. Dickson appeared to be a big man wearing dark clothes, with long hair that went down nearly to his shoulders. As he watched, a waiter came up with a tray of food, setting it on the table in front of the trio. Virgil knew at that moment he'd found the man they were supposed to kill. He also knew exactly where he would be for at least the next hour. Ike had said to meet back in one hour. That hour was up. He started quickly across the street, heading for the alley that would take him to his brothers with news they all wanted to hear.

'I got 'em.' Virgil ran up to the shadowy figures of his brothers. 'He's over at the Palace eatin' dinner with them two mine men right now. When he comes out we gotta be ready to kill 'em!'

'Should we take him on the street, or

when he starts back to Birdie's?' Elwood wondered out loud.

'Better on the street where we got some light,' Ike ordered. 'It's too dark goin' back to her place.'

'What about them mine men, what if they get in the way?' Emmett questioned.

'Then we take them down too so we can get a clear shot at Dickson. He's the only one carryin' a pistol. Four against one is my kind of odds in a dog fight,' Ike continued. 'Here's how we'll do it. Emmett an' me will wait right across the street so we can see him when he comes out. Let 'em get all the way out on the boardwalk. Elwood, you git down the street just a few feet away up against the building. You'll have a clear shot at his back. Virgil, you git yourself in that alley next to the Palace. You'll have a head-on shot if he tries to run for it. After the first shot, everyone open up on him and be sure you kill him. I don't want him runnin' away without bleeding out. You all know what you're supposed to do?' All three nodded. 'Then let's git to it!'

Throughout their long dinner, Dickson and the mine men discussed the Goss family and how Dickson would handle the whole bunch when the brothers returned from Fool's Gold, if in fact they had ever left. Rolo said the old man would lie through his teeth to save his boys, and think nothing of it. He repeated that it didn't make any sense the brothers would ride that far. He couldn't think of any reason they would. Chambers added wherever the four were, they were always dangerous and unpredictable, driven by the iron will of their father. The three men finished dinner with one more glass of whiskey, before Chambers hailed the waiter over to pay the bill.

'It's been an interesting evening.' Dickson got to his feet as Rolo and Edward followed. 'I wanted as much information as I could get, and you've given me that. I'll use it tomorrow when I ride back out to their ranch.'

'You still plan on going alone?' Rolo questioned.

'I do. That's how I always deal with people like that, face to face when they least expect it. Most men caught short don't have time to react. If there's trouble, I'll make the first move to end it. This bunch will be no different than anyone else.'

Rolo slowly shook his head, marvelling at Dickson's determination. 'Don't be too sure about that. They're backwoods people who have no regard for anyone else except themselves. I wouldn't put trying to kill you past any of them, and you'll likely be facing more than just one of them. I'm convinced that's what they did to John Standard.'

The three men walked out of the dining room through the busy bar, stepping out on to the boardwalk. Dickson was in the lead with Rolo and Edward right behind him. Dickson stopped a moment to flare a match, lighting a pencil-thin cigarillo. Elwood stepped away from the building drawing his pistol, but the mine men blocked his view. Across the street Ike and Emmett lifted their six-guns trying to get a clear shot at the knot of men as they talked for a moment. In the alley, Virgil peeked around the corner waiting for his brothers to shoot before he opened up. When they did not he backed away from the edge, wondering why. Elwood became more nervous and confused every second until he couldn't wait any longer. 'Dickson!' he yelled, as the three men turned around to his sudden shout.

Dickson instantly shoved Rolo and Edward out of the way and crouched, pulling his Colt. Elwood took a wild shot that missed. Dickson's six-gun bucked in his hands spitting flame and lead, collapsing Elwood on the board-walk with a scream of pain rolling out into the street. Ike and Emmett instantly began firing wildly from across the street.

'Get down!' Dickson yelled, pushing

the pair behind a watering trough in front of the Palace. The brothers' bullets thudded into the tank, sending sudden geysers of water into the air. Virgil stepped out of the alley levelling his pistol on Dickson, firing as fast as he could thumb the hammer. One bullet hit Dickson's wooden leg, jerking it out from under him. He instinctively rolled over on his stomach, firing back with two fast shots. Rolo yelled out, hit in the arm by a bullet. Virgil jumped back into the alley for cover as Dickson's bullets splintered the corner inches away. Elwood continued dragging himself across the street, moaning for someone to help him. Ike screamed at Emmett to go pull his brother out of harm's way, while he continued shooting at the three behind the trough.

Inside the Palace, people dove for the floor as stray bullets shattered the front window and the big mirror behind the bar came crashing down. The bartender dropped to his knees, grabbing the shotgun he kept under the bar and a handful of shotgun shells, cussing out loud while running for the front door. A quick peek outside showed his previous diners were outnumbered with Ike and Emmett firing steadily from across the street. The barman lifted the 12 gauge firing both barrels, forcing the pair to drop to the ground as pellets shattered store windows behind them.

'Let's git outta here!' Emmett pleaded. 'We can't take on a scattergun too!'

'Grab Elwood and let's go!' Ike yelled as Emmett made a run for it, dragging his brother back. Both men lifted Elwood between them, running down the boardwalk toward the alley behind, horses jittering at the hitching post from the thunderous gun fire.

Virgil saw his brothers run for it. Instantly he realized he was on his own. Turning, he ran down the alley as fast as his legs would carry him. As suddenly as the furious gunfight began, it ended. Dickson slowly got to his feet, unsteady on just one leg. He turned to see Edward helping Rolo to his feet, a bloody bullet wound on the fleshy part of his arm. People poured out of the Palace on to the boardwalk, talking excitedly.

'Someone get a doctor!' Dickson yelled. 'We've got a wounded man here.'

'What about you?' Chambers asked. 'You'll need one too.'

Dickson lifted his pants leg showing the shattered bullet hole through his wooden leg, as Chambers' eyes widened in disbelief. 'Well I'll be damned,' he exclaimed. 'I never knew you had a false leg.'

'Had it for years. This is the first time it saved me from the real thing though. I'll have to get a new one made before I ride out to the Goss ranch. That's who tried to ambush us. There's no doubt about that. They've started the war. Now I'll finish it.'

'You're right, Ben. I heard the one you wounded calling out for Ike and Emmett. You better take some help with you before you go out to their ranch, after all this. They'll open up on you the minute you show your face, Ben.'

'I'll take some help all right. I'll have a little surprise with me. You use dynamite, don't you?'

'Sure we do in our hard rock mining. Why do you ask?'

'I want several sticks and fuses, too.'

'What for? It's dangerous stuff to play around with.'

'I don't want to play around with it. I'll stop by your office in the morning after I get this leg of mine fixed and pick it up.'

'You ever handled dynamite before?'

'I have. Used it once down in New Mexico, to smoke out some train robbers I had cornered in a cave. I might need it to smoke out the Goss boys, too.'

★   ★   ★

Vernal Goss slumped in his chair in the dark of the front room waiting, listening for his boys' return from town. His

67

stomach churned as beads of perspiration broke out on his white-whiskered face. Closing his eyes for a moment he tried to overcome the nausea of fear, slowly rocking back and forth in the chair. He wasn't about to be pushed any further by this lawman Ben Dickson, but there was always a chance his dangerous plan to ambush him could have gone wrong. The longer he waited for the boys to show up the more uncertain and agitated he became. His tremors returned, shaking him from head to toe so badly the chair vibrated on the wooden floor, sounding like a baby's rattle.

'Vernal . . . are you . . . all right?' Hattie's sleepy voice drifted out from the back bedroom. 'Are the . . . boys back yet? I can't get much sleep worrying about them.'

He grit his teeth, trying to answer. 'No they ain't. I'll let you know when. Go back to sleep and stop askin' me dumb questions!'

Another long hour ticked slowly away on the clock on the stone fireplace mantle, when Vernal suddenly straightened up. He thought he heard the sound of distant hoof beats coming fast. Cupping a hand to his ear he strained to hear it again. It was getting closer. Was it his boys or not? Horses danced to a stop outside. Vernal cocked back both hammers on his double barrel shotgun, levelling it on the front door. If it wasn't his boys but Dickson or maybe even a posse, he'd end the battle right here and now with both barrels before they took him down.

'Paw, it's us. We got Elwood and he's hurt bad!' Ike's frantic voice cut through the night like a knife. 'We're comin' in!'

The brothers half dragged Elwood through the door, laying him on the couch as Ike called out for someone to light the coal oil lamp. Hattie ran in in her nightgown, hand over mouth at Ike's desperate shouts. The lamp flickered to life as she knelt at Elwood's side, trying to comfort him.

'How bad is it, son? Let me see what happened to my boy.' Her tiny voice quavered with emotion.

She lifted his bloody shirt, her face twisting in revulsion at what she saw. Tears instantly welled up in her eyes.

'Well, can you help him or is he gonna die right here?' Vernal barked, twisting in the chair, trying to get a better look.

'Looks like . . . the bullet went clean through . . . his side . . . maybe caught part of his stomach. All I can do is try to stop the bleeding . . . maybe sew it up some. One of you boys go to the kitchen quick and get me that bottle of whiskey so I can wash it . . . out.'

'Did you kill Dickson?' Vernal demanded.

'I know I hit him, Paw. He could be bleedin' out right now. I saw him go down!' Virgil insisted.

'What about you and Emmett, Ike? Did you get some lead in him?'

'We opened up on him when that barman from the Palace ran out with a scattergun and cut loose on us with both barrels. We couldn't take on a

70

six-gun and a shotgun, too. We had to get Elwood out of there. All we could do is run for it.'

'Run for it? You were supposed to kill him. You sure no one followed you out here?'

'We didn't see no one. We was pretty busy just tryin' to get here ourselves.'

The old man lowered his head in one hand, shaking it at the mess the boys had made of his plans. He had to think up something else and fast before either Dickson or a posse came riding out to take the boys in and maybe him too. He looked at Elwood twisting and moaning as Hattie swabbed his bullet wound with whiskey, then back to his sons as his mind struggled for an answer. There was only one thing he could think of to save all of them, dangerous as it seemed.

'C'm'ere you three.' He waved them over. 'You listen to me and listen good. Sooner or later either Dickson, if he ain't dead, or maybe more men from town are gonna come out here looking

71

for all three of you. There's only one way I can think of to save you. That's for all of you to light out away from here. If you ain't here there's nothing anyone can do about it.'

'Leave for where?' Virgil questioned, eyes wide with fear.

'On over the mountains past Fool's Gold, the country drops down into a place they called the badlands, when I was a kid. The wagon trains still go around it because it's so rough. It's all chopped up with a million canyons and box canyons. No one can track you once you get in there. Even the Indians stay out of it. They think it's full of demons ridin' on the wind. No one here is gonna go that far lookin' for you, either. That's the only kinda place you'll be safe. After all this dies down you can come back home.'

'How far is it from here, and when can we come back home?' Ike wondered out loud.

'I ain't sure. Maybe three or four months. Maybe even longer. It's a hundred miles or so from here. You'll have to take as much supplies as you can pack and shoot something to eat when that runs out. That's all I can think of.'

The brothers stared at each other, too stunned to reply for several moments until Emmett found his voice.

'What about Elwood? He can't ride shot up like he is!'

'You'll have to take him, too. If anyone finds him here with that bullet wound they'll know fer sure it was you who tried to gun down Dickson. If you boys had done the job right you wouldn't have to run for it. Now that's the only chance you got left!'

'But Paw, it was all we could do just getting Elwood here. There ain't no way he could ride a hundred miles,' Virgil challenged.

'He'll have to and so will you!'

'What if he dies on the trail?' Ike's voice was near panic.

'You got no choice. It's the only way to save yourselves. And it's better than all of you dyin' at the end of a rope. Get some supplies together and fast. Your mother will try and make Elwood ready to ride. If you have to rope him in the saddle, do it!'

4

The crowds in front of the Palace slowly began dispersing with everyone still talking excitedly about the wild shootout. Rolo was taken to the doctor's office between the shoulders of Edward and a volunteer from the crowd. Dickson turned to the barman whose sudden intervention had turned the tide of the gunfight in his favour.

'That double barrel of yours did good work. I'm a shotgun man myself and know those twin barrels have a way of stopping anyone dead in their tracks. Thanks for your help.'

'Listen, I'm no gunman or anything like it, but after having my front window shot out and the big mirror behind the bar smashed to pieces, I had to do something. I couldn't let that go on. One of my customers might have caught a bullet. That mirror had to be freight-hauled all the way up from Denver, and it cost plenty. All it is now is a pile of broken glass. Who's got it in for you so bad they'd try to kill you right here out on Main Street?'

'Maybe you can get the Goss brothers to pay for all the glass. They're the ones who did the shooting.'

'Those animals? Are you that sure?'

'I am. There's no doubt in my mind.'

'If they show their faces here in my place again I'll put this shotgun back on them and make them pay for all the damage they've done.'

'They might not be around long enough to do that.'

'Why's that?'

'I'm going to pay them a little visit after I get my leg fixed. You know a good carpenter in town?'

'Yeah, there's Delbert Combs, one block over from here. He has a shop out on the side of his house. When I need work done here in the Palace, I use him. He's real good with wood. What's that got to do with your leg?'

Dickson lifted his pants leg, revealing the shattered bullet hole.

'Ain't that something. I would have never guessed you had a peg leg. I'll bet Delbert is just the man to make you a new one.'

'I'll find out tomorrow soon as he opens. I've got to get this replaced before I settle things out at the Goss ranch. That little ride will take two good legs, not one.'

* * *

'You want what?' Delbert Combs turned from his workbench next morning as Dickson entered his shop with a quick hello, followed by a request.

'I need this replaced.' He lifted his pants leg again, revealing the splintered hole. 'And I need it done perfectly so it fits snug in my boot, including the shape of my foot. If it isn't done right my balance will be off and I can't have that.'

Combs adjusted his glasses, running

a hand through thinning hair, studying the tall man then looking down at the leg. 'I've done a lot of different jobs before but never anything like that. I'm not a doctor, you know.'

'If you don't think you can handle it I'll have to find someone else,' Dickson challenged. 'I'm told you're the man good with tools.'

'I didn't say I couldn't do it. Only that it's darned unusual. When would you need it finished?'

'Today. I can't leave here without it. I'd have to stay right here until you're done.'

Combs was silent a moment longer trying to figure out how much time and material he had to work with. 'I do have a good piece of seasoned oak over in the wood rack that might work pretty well and I'd have to use your old leg for a pattern.' He pulled at his chin, thinking it over. 'All right, take it off and I'll get started on it. You may as well find a comfortable seat. You're going to be here a while.'

Combs went to work measuring the leg before rough sawing the oak and heading for his pedal wheel lathe to begin turning the hardwood block down to specifications. Dickson sat quietly on a three-legged stool, watching the old craftsman diligently working at his craft when his wife Amanda came into the shop with a pot of hot black coffee.

'I saw you had an early customer Del, so I made up a pot of coffee for both of you.' She eyed Dickson curiously with his fine clothes and fancy lace-up boots. He looked so out of place in a rough mining town like Peralta, that she couldn't take her eyes off him. She poured two cups, handing one to Dickson, but Delbert was too busy to stop.

'Thank you, ma'am. That's very perceptive of you. This should take the chill off the morning air.' He tipped his big brimmed hat.

'Yes, it is turning toward fall, and that will come . . . ' She glanced down at

Dickson's empty pants leg and boot, suddenly stopping her remarks, embarrassed for not noticing. 'Please excuse me. I didn't know . . . '

'That's quite all right mam. Most people are taken back a bit at first. It's nothing really to apologize for. Don't think anything of it. I certainly don't. My name is Ben Dickson. I'm staying here in town for a short while and maybe just a little bit longer until your husband finishes with my new leg,' he kidded.

'Can I assume you're a businessman, Mr Dickson? You certainly dress like one.'

'Yes, I do have a business of sorts.'

'Do you mind me asking what that is?'

'No, not one bit. I'm a hunter, ma'am.'

'A hunter? How interesting. It must pay very well.'

'Yes it does, most of the time.'

'Amanda, will you stop asking questions and leave my customer alone.'

Delbert's voice had a tinge of frustration in it, without turning toward her.

Her face flushed at his rebuke. 'I am sorry. Delbert is right. I've got plenty to do in the house. Enjoy your stay, Mr Dickson. I'm certain my husband will do an excellent job for you. If you're still here at noon, I'll bring both of you something to eat too.'

The afternoon sun touched the jagged line of timber tops behind Peralta, when Ben Dickson stepped outside Delbert Combs' wood shop, testing his new leg. He paused, hands at his side, relaxing as Combs came to the door surveying his handiwork.

'Well, how does the new leg feel?' he asked.

'I'll let you know in a moment.'

Dickson stood stock still before suddenly pulling his pearl-handled six-gun, crouching slightly, testing his balance. The move was so fast and smooth it took Combs completely by surprise.

'I'd say it feels all right. You did a good job.'

Combs didn't answer for several seconds as his mind raced about this unusual man he'd made a new leg for. He'd seen what he thought was a courteous customer with a serious disability turn into a man who measured his new balance and speed by pulling a a big Colt. Something his wife had mentioned earlier came back to him.

'You told Amanda you were a hunter, didn't you Mr Dickson?'

'I did at that.' Dickson turned back to the wood worker, sliding the .45 back in its holster. 'You didn't exactly say what it was you hunted, did you?'

'No, I did not out of respect for her sensibilities.'

'Would you be . . . a man hunter? You mentioned riding out to the Goss ranch when I finished with your leg. Most folks around here know they're nothing but trouble.'

'I am. I carry a marshal's badge to back me up wherever I go.'

Delbert eyed the tall man, thinking something over. 'Seems quite a while back, I heard the name Ben Dickson before. He lived way down south near desert country. I didn't connect it with you until I saw you pull that fancy pistol of yours. Are you one and the same, Mr Dickson?'

'Yes, Mr Combs. Now tell me what I owe you for this superb job you did on my leg, and I'll be on my way out to the Goss ranch.'

By the time Dickson walked down to the livery stable to saddle his horse, the Goss brothers were already miles away, well up into the mountains riding fast on a narrow trail threading its way higher through thick timber. Ike led with Emmett right behind him and Virgil farther back, trying to encourage Elwood to keep up. His bullet wound was bleeding again and the throbbing pain in his stomach was so excruciating all he could do was lean low and hang on to the saddle horn, as Virgil pulled his horse by its reins. As they neared another ridge top, Ike turned, yelling back, 'What's holdin' you up, Virgil? We can't slow down now!'

'Elwood can't keep up. He's real bad off. We might have to stop and give him a rest.'

'I ain't stoppin' for no one. We gotta keep goin' as hard as we can. If he can't keep up, cut 'em loose. He'll have to catch up to us later. There might be a whole posse comin' after us. I'm gonna ride through the night just to be sure we stay ahead.'

Virgil looked back at his brother, head down, eyes closed. He was torn between staying with him or obeying Ike's order.

'Elwood . . . Elwood, can you hear me? I'm going to have to let you make your own way, understand? Let your horse follow us. You won't have to lead him. Just give him his head. I'm sorry, brother. I don't have no choice in this. I've got to keep up with Ike and Emmett. We'll all meet in Fool's Gold, tomorrow. You have to hang on until then. Try, brother, just try.'

Virgil kicked his horse away higher

until all three riders disappeared up the trail, reaching top country half an hour later when they pulled to a halt, giving the horses a blow. The guilt of leaving his brother behind still plagued Virgil.

'Elwood isn't going to make it. Maybe if he does catch up we should tell him to try and get back home where at least Mom can doctor him some,' he suggested, looking to Ike and Emmett for support.

'He can do what he has to, but we ain't waitin' for him. He went and got himself shot, and I ain't gonna slip my neck through a hangman's noose pullin' him along with me so someone can catch up to us. Those badlands Paw talked about are someplace over these mountains past Fool's Gold. We don't even know how far. He said maybe a hundred miles or more from home. If we can get there ain't no one going to follow us that far. That's the only real chance we got and I ain't losin' it over Elwood or anyone else. Now let's get kicking!'

Vernal Goss barely slept after the boys left and Hattie retreated to the bedroom, burying her head in the covers, crying quietly so he couldn't hear her. She'd pleaded with Vernal not to send Elwood with his brothers, but he wouldn't listen to her. He never listened. She was wracked with fear she'd never see Elwood again — maybe none of the boys. Her frail body lay in bed, thinking about all the misery her mule-headed husband had visited on the entire family. She was certain he'd be the death of them all sooner or later and there was nothing she could do to stop him. His sudden shout made her jump.

'Hattie, get yourself in here and help me try to get to my feet. And stop that blubberin' too. I can still hear it!'

She came into the room, drying her eyes as he waved her closer.

'Where do you want to go, Vernal?'

'Out on the front porch. Help me up.'

'It's freezing cold outside. Why go out there, Vernal?'

'Because if someone is comin' here, I want to face them out there, not in here. Now stop askin' stupid questions and try to help me up.'

Hattie struggled with getting her arms under him, barely able to keep herself upright pulling him out of the chair as he wove unsteady on dead stumps. Vernal grabbed the chair with one hand for support, wrapping the other over her shoulder as they stumbled out on to the porch. After retrieving the chair, Vernal dropped heavily into it with another demand.

'Get me a good blanket and my shotgun too. I'm spendin' the night right here in case someone is fool enough to show up and wants some double barrel trouble. Then get yourself back inside and close the door. Don't open it unless you hear me callin' for you.'

★   ★   ★

Dickson rode slowly through the night, knowing if the Goss brothers were at the ranch, he'd be facing more than just one gun. He'd already made plans for that. That's one reason he chose to show up after dark. Nighttime was his ally. It gave him cover and masked any fast moves he might have to make. He knew the boys and the old man were not face to face gunfighters like others he'd faced in the past. They were back shooters and alley ambushers. That gave him another important edge, plus the dynamite he carried in his saddlebags made the odds closer. Whatever happened he was either bringing those boys in with their bodies roped over horses, or at the end of his shotgun.

Dickson pulled his horse to a halt at the edge of the canyon across from the old ranch house, quietly studying the scene for several moments. No lamplight flickered through darkened windows, no horses were tied out front. He pulled his short-barrelled shotgun out of its scabbard, resting it across his lap before easing his horse forward again down the steep canyon-side hill.

Vernal Goss had stared into the night a long time thinking about his sons and how far away they might be by now. He'd never admit it out loud, but he knew his plan to ambush and kill Ben Dickson had ended up being a disaster. He kept trying to excuse its failure, convincing himself if the boys had done what he'd ordered none of this would have happened in the first place. The more he thought about it, the more convinced he became was he was right. It was all the boys' fault, not his.

As time passed and the night grew colder he wondered who, if anyone, would be riding out to confront him. If there was going to be a gunfight he was ready for it. He was sick and tired of being a hopeless cripple who couldn't help himself and always needed the boys or Hattie to do everything for him.

All he had left was his maniacal pride that no one dared walk on the Goss name and get away with it. He'd made that stick, cripple or not. If there was going to be a shootout maybe even death wouldn't be so bad, considering the way he'd had to live all these years since the accident. If he went down shooting, at least town people would say he died like a real man.

His thoughts were suddenly interrupted by the sound of a horse's hooves coming slowly up the hill toward the house. He pulled himself straight up in the chair, wiping his eyes, thumbing back both hammers on the shotgun, peering into the dark, trying to see who it was. The shadowed image of a horse came closer. He lifted the shotgun to his shoulder, his finger tightening on the trigger.

'Whoever you are, stop right there or I'll blow you out of that saddle!' Vernal's shout shattered the night as he leaned closer trying to get a better look, the horse stopping only yards away.

That's when he realized there was no one in the saddle.

'What the hell?' He lowered the shotgun, squinting harder at the strange sight.

The tiniest squeak on the porch boards behind him was instantly followed by the icy feel of shotgun barrels pressed hard against the back of his head. Ben Dickson leaned closer, whispering in his ear.

'Lift that shotgun of yours up real slow by the barrels with one hand. If I see two coming up you won't even have time to blink!'

The old man jerked convulsively, caught by complete surprise. The steel tubes pressed harder against his shaggy white hair. Vernal lifted the scattergun over his shoulder until Dickson took it.

'That's better. Now where are those bushwhacking boys of yours? I want a straight answer and I want it quick.'

'They . . . ain't here you back stabbin' bastard!'

'If I go in the house and find them,

I'm going to dynamite this place to pieces for lying to me. Then I'll take all five of you into town. By now people in Peralta will be ready to hang the whole bunch of you.'

'I said they ain't here and they ain't!'

'Then where are they?'

'They're . . . off someplace. I don't know where. Git that damn shotgun off the back of my head!'

Dickson straightened up, lifting the shotgun before walking around to face the old man. 'You keep your mouth shut and don't make a sound. I'm going in. You better hope I don't find any of them.'

'My wife Hattie is the only one inside and she's asleep. Leave her alone. She don't know nothin' anyway.'

Dickson eased the front door open cautiously, stepping inside, standing for a few moments as his eyes adjusted to the dark. In meagre light he made out the glassy reflection of a coal oil lamp sitting atop of the fireplace mantel. Crossing the room he removed the lamp chimney, lighting the wick. The soft glow lit the shabby room, exposing a hallway leading further into the house. He started down it over creaking floors until coming to the first bedroom on the right. Quietly twisting the knob he stepped inside, lifting the light with one hand, levelling the shotgun with the other. Blankets lay scattered across the floor. Over against one wall a broken down dresser with most drawers pulled out was empty. The unkempt bed was empty too. He exited the room, tiptoeing to a second door on the opposite side of the hall. Stepping quietly inside, the lamp lit a pair of bunk beds on the wall. Scattered clothes were piled on the empty beds and several shelves were also in disarray. It was clear the Goss boys were gone and had left in a big hurry. He exited the bedroom, stepping outside to see a final closed door at the end of the darkened hall.

Dickson paused a moment, quietly turning the handle, stepping inside, shotgun levelled on what the lamp light revealed. Under a pile of blankets at the far end of the room, a form moved slightly followed by the sound of uneven breathing. Easing forward one slow step at a time he crossed the room. At the bed he slowly lifted the covers only to see an old, grey-haired woman with a wrinkled face moaning something as she tried to open her eyes to wake up.

'Vernal . . . how did you . . . get in here?' She sleepily pulled herself up on one elbow, shielding her eyes from the sudden light with her other hand.

'I'm not Vernal. My name is Ben Dickson. I'm a US deputy marshal looking for your sons. Where are they? If you don't give me a straight answer I'll take your husband into town and lock him up until I find them. Answer me.'

Hattie closed her eyes, slowly shaking her head in confusion. She didn't know what to say or who this demanding voice behind the lamp light was. 'Where is . . . Vernal?' she finally asked.

'He's out front without the shotgun he meant to use on me. I want to know where your boys went. It's clear they left here in a hurry, and it had to be sometime tonight. Tell me the truth or your husband can hang for trying to have them kill me. I know all about that. Now talk.'

Cornered and confused, she didn't know how to answer. The demands came too fast. Lifting both hands she closed her eyes, cradling her head in despair. Dickson knew she was his best chance to get the information he needed. He decided on one more tactic to break her. 'If I can take your boys without a gunfight, I will. But know that sooner or later I'm going find them with or without your help. If I have to do it on my own, it will go harder on them and your husband too. You can still save them if you tell me what you know and right now.'

She took in a long breath, trying to calm herself. Tears began running down her face knowing what fate her entire family might be in for. She'd tried to tell Vernal not to go ahead with his wild plans to kill Dickson, and now it had all fallen apart and come to this. If Vernal wouldn't try to save her sons, then she was the only person left who could. She couldn't hold out any longer.

'My boys . . . went over to Fool's Gold. That's all I know about it.'

'How far is that from here?'

'I don't know. I've never been there. I only heard Vernal tell the boys to go there. It's over the mountains some-place to the east. If you find them, tell them I prayed for them to come home safe and not use guns anymore. Tell them I want them to set things right with the law.'

Dickson stared down at the emotionally-drained old woman. He knew he'd gotten as much as he could out of her. Exiting the room, he could hear the sounds of her crying all the way down the hall. Once out on the porch he stopped briefly to confront the old man. 'I know where your boys are going and I'm going after them. When I get back if I hear you laid so much as one hand on your wife, I'll come back out here and beat you within an inch of your life, cripple or not. Remember what I said. I mean every word of it!'

Vernal's hands gripped the chair in bone-white defiance, but he wasn't done yet.

'You shoulda killed me when you had the chance, 'cause I'll kill you if you ever show your law-dog face around here again!'

'You just might get that chance. I'll look forward to it. You've already caused enough misery and murder to everyone including your own family. Your time is done, old man, and I'll end it for you without a second thought.'

5

Dickson rode back into town, stabling his horse and checking on the packer. He'd need both early tomorrow when he rode out after the brothers. A short night's sleep at Birdie Lee's boarding house was all he'd get and maybe a little information from her. She seemed to know everything about everyone in town, maybe she'd also know something about Fool's Gold too. Rolo and Edward were already closed up this late so he'd leave a note on their door telling them he was going after the brothers and where. They were both paying the bill to bring the murderers back to face justice. He wanted to let them know why he wouldn't be back in town for a while.

Reaching the boarding house he was surprised to see Birdie still up, working in the kitchen. 'Why would you want to go way up there at this time of the year? That high country around Fool's Gold can get early snow about now,' she questioned, cocking her head.

'It's business, madam. Do you know where the trail starts here?' He wasn't about to go into details with her but Birdie suddenly had another worry and it wasn't about the way to Fool's Gold.

'If you're leaving, you won't be needing your room anymore. You couldn't get up there and back before your rent would be due again.'

'I'm keeping my room, and I'll pay you for two weeks in advance. That way you won't have to worry about your precious money. And I still do not want anyone going into my room while I'm gone. Do I make myself clear on that, Miss Lee? Now can you direct me to the trailhead to Fool's Gold, or not?'

Birdie stiffened for a moment at being talked to like a child, but recovered quick enough. 'I'm told it's only a horse trail. It's too rugged and not wide enough for wagon travel. It starts out just outside town. There's an old weathered signboard marking it. I hear it's a good two days' ride just to get there. Does that answer your question, Mr Dickson?'

'It does madam. I'll be up and gone before you so I'll pay you now for the room.'

True to his word, next morning Dickson rode down the quiet streets of Peralta, to darkened store fronts and empty boardwalks. Only the light from the Palace and a smaller gambling house across the street cast a faint glow on to the street. Beyond the last buildings he found the wooden sign pointing up into shadowed timber. Urging his horse up the trail he pulled the packer behind him.

An hour later as dawn came over the land, he rode out on to an open saddle clear of timber. Looking far down the canyon he recognized the tiny structure that was the Goss ranch situated on a steep-sided hill. Hattie's admission that her sons had ridden for Fool's Gold made even more sense now with the trail passing so close above the old house. Ahead, the trail continued to climb into thick timber gaining elevation. He pulled his jacket collar higher against the morning chill before pulling deerskin gloves tighter over his hands. At least Birdie was right about something. Fall was coming fast to this high country.

★ ★ ★

Ike, Virgil and Emmett kicked their horses hard all that day, weaving in and out of dog-hair timber. Every time Emmett looked back to see if Elwood was in sight all he saw was an empty trail, worrying him even more about his brother's fate. 'Why don't we give the horses a breather and see if Elwood can catch up?' he shouted to Ike in the lead.

'We'll give 'em a break when I say so!' he yelled back over his shoulder, already irritated that Emmett had asked him the same question every half hour. Emmett bit his lip, torn between keeping up or stopping to help his brother.

The four of them had always done every-thing together and stood up for each other no matter how bad things got. Now Ike and Virgil didn't care if Elwood died on the trail or got captured by anyone following them. He couldn't under-stand why everything had changed so suddenly.

'If you was wounded I'd stop to help you out!' he shouted back in frustration.

'Well I ain't wounded and I still ain't stoppin', so don't ask me again. You wanna turn back, go ahead. But if a posse or Dickson catches up to you don't go cryin' you got left behind. You did it to your own self, not me or Virgil. One more day and we'll be in Fool's Gold. You can wait for him there, not out here!'

* * *

The tall man rode steadily throughout that day until late afternoon, when the sun began sliding down toward arrow-topped pines. He reined his horse off the trail into a thick stand of white-barked quaking aspen. The cool afternoon wind fluttered their golden leaves, blinking bright with colour. After unsaddling his horse he unloaded the canvas manti on the packer, hobbling both animals to feed on nearby greenery at the edge of the trees. He knew the Goss brothers had nearly a full day's head start on him. But he also knew that Elwood was wounded. He wasn't at the Goss ranch, so he had to be riding with his brothers. How long he could do that before it got so unbearable he'd have to stop had to be a plus on Dickson's side. That could slow or maybe even erase any lead the brothers had on him.

Dickson spread out his warm eider-down bedroll before retrieving hard tack and venison jerky from one of his saddle-bags for dinner. There would be no fire tonight or on any other night, as long as he trailed the brothers. He learned long ago even a small fire could be seen from miles away. He'd take no chance that might happen. It was an iron clad rule he never violated while hunting down anyone.

* * *

Nighttime spread its icy cloak over Elwood too, but a far crueler one. What little strength he had left was fading fast. Every step his horse took and every breath he drew was a dagger pain stabbing deep in his stomach. His brothers had abandoned him and he was too weak to turn around and try to ride back home. He pulled his horse to a stop, slowly sliding out of the saddle and sinking to the ground, crawling up against a tree for support. Frantic and delirious, he told himself to try and meet death like a man. Feebly pulling his pistol he brought the gun up into his lap, covering it with both hands. If someone did show up, at least he'd have the chance to take him out with him. His Paw would be proud to hear he'd done that. As temperatures sank further he began shivering uncontrollably. He needed a fire badly and even though he had matches, he was too weak to gather any wood. All Elwood Goss could do was curl up in a ball and whimper like a child.

* * *

Dickson was up very early, as was his usual habit when trailing men. He'd perfected his craft over many years facing down those that didn't want to be found. Some of those men killed from ambush and bragged about it later, drinking too much tongue oil. Others did it stone-cold sober to intimidate those around them, lesser men who liked rubbing shoulders with danger, without ever facing it themselves with a pistol in their hands. Dickson could size up what kind of men he faced in the first three seconds of a showdown. The quiet ones without bravado or bluster, who instantly squared off against him, were the most dangerous. They meant to match their speed and killing-gun handling to come out on top. The talkers who threatened and made wild gestures were just plain scared and easily taken. A pistol smash over the head was all that was needed to subdue them. He'd only had half a minute of wild gunfire facing the Goss brothers that night in front of the Palace, and their inept attempt to ambush him. They might be far different men face to face and with the gun odds on their side. He thought about all this saddling up his horse while roping supplies back on the packer. Climbing into a squeaky saddle, he reined the horses back out on the trail. Hattie had said she thought Fool's Gold was about two days' ride away. If she was right, he might reach it with only one night on the trail. That could be a big 'if', with the brothers someplace between him and town.

The narrow trail that morning levelled out from all the climbing the previous day. Several little springs Dickson crossed were all frozen icy white. Even scattered trees bent at odd angles began to show the limit of timber and heavy snows of winter that had shaped them. The riding was easier now but not so easy that Dickson let himself relax into a false sense of security. The morning passed uneventfully under a weak sun reaching its zenith behind a thin layer of high herringbone clouds, before Dickson pulled to a sudden stop, getting down. Peering closer, he found a blotch of dried blood. Leading his horse a few yards ahead, he found another, then another. It had to be Elwood, and if he was bleeding out that bad he couldn't be that far ahead. Mounting again, he slid the shotgun from its scabbard. He didn't want any sudden surprises without a fast double barrel reply.

Dickson decided the smartest thing to do now was not to ride into an ambush staying on the trail. Instead, he reined his horse off, parallelling it, picking his way through scattered timber, but where he could still see the path off to his right. If Goss was still alive he'd be waiting for anyone following him trying to get in the first shot. Each copse of trees ahead and every turn where Elwood could be hiding, Dickson avoided by getting down, leaving his horse while he moved ahead on foot, studying every shadow and clump of cover. As he cleared each one, he whistled his horse to join him.

He followed this careful procedure into mid-afternoon when he came to another cluster of trees on a bend in the trail. Dismounting, Dickson eased forward quietly, eyes searching for any shape or form out of place, stepping inside the piney tangle. He stopped, listening for any sound that shouldn't be there. Nothing stirred. Moving ahead one slow step, he suddenly saw Elwood's horse beyond the trees, standing unattended, head down nibbling short grass. Elwood had to be right here, someplace very close. A tingle of anticipation made the hair on the back of his neck stand out as it always did when gunplay was only seconds away. Very quietly he cocked the hammers back on both barrels of the shotgun, taking another few steps before seeing a pair of boots sticking out behind a large pine tree just ahead. If Elwood was right handed as most men were, Dickson knew it would take him a half second longer to roll up from a sitting position to lift a pistol and shoot to his right. Dickson eased up to the big tree, lowering the scattergun, stepping halfway around to see Elwood propped up against the trunk, eyes closed, half conscious. Suddenly he opened them in terror, being caught by surprise. The shotgun roared before Elwood lifted the pistol off his lap, rolling him on the ground, screaming in pain, doubling up. Dickson stepped closer, kicking the wheel gun away.

'Where are your brothers?' he demanded, leaning down, rolling Elwood over. 'Are they in Fool's Gold? Answer me while you can. You're done for. You may as well do one decent thing before you're gone!'

Elwood's mouth moved but no words

came out, only the desperate gasps of a man at the door of eternity. He had just enough strength left to reach up, pulling Dickson down nearly face to face. 'Tell . . . momma . . . I'll meet her at the . . . golden gates of glory . . . while you're . . . in hell.'

Elwood's hand dropped to his side and his eyes faded to a cold, lifeless stare. Dickson straightened up to his feet, looking down on the bloody mess of a man. Maybe, he thought, Elwood's dying words might be true. Maybe he would end up in hell for all the men he'd killed and the misery he'd inflicted on their families. One thing Dickson was certain of, when he drew his last breath he wouldn't be calling out for a mother he hardly knew. She was someone who had a reputation for being more a 'woman of town' than she ever was his mother. He knew even less about his father. He could have been a gunfighter, lawman, or farmer who broke his back all his life over dirt clods and crops. At this point in his life it mattered little. He knew what he was and what he did for a living.

Dickson went through Elwood's jacket and pants pockets, retrieving an old beat-up pocket watch, a few dollars in coins and a blood-splattered picture of Vernal and Hattie. He studied the few items in his hands. Was this all a man's life came down to in the end? He could put it in one pocket. He'd done a lot of killing and never thought much about the men he'd killed or why. He was paid and paid well to do it. Motive didn't really matter. The men who went down in front of his guns would have done the same thing to him if they'd been just a hair faster. Why, he wondered, was he even asking those questions after all these years, and over a poor wretch of a man who didn't stand a chance against him or much of anyone else either? Elwood Goss was no gunfighter. He was propped up by his father's rage and his brothers' presence. Alone he was a pathetic figure. Any two-bit saloon braggart could have taken him down. As far as Ike, Virgil and Emmett went, that was a different concern. Dickson's sixth sense warned him they would pull a trigger as quick as look at him. He'd have to deal with them in a much different way.

He took the time to cut pine boughs, placing them over Elwood's body. If someone wanted to find him and take him home, his small effort might keep the wolves and bears off him for a little while. The next stop was Fool's Gold. Maybe he'd find the remaining brothers there. He knew that would be a showdown far different from this one.

* * *

Ike, Virgil and Emmett rode out of timber, pulling to a halt looking down on the small but lively town of Fool's Gold. Emmett couldn't stop worrying about Elwood. How far back was he by now, and how long would it take for him to catch up? If he did, maybe he could find a horse doctor to help him out. He took the chance to question Ike again.

'What are we going to do now, Ike? Can we rest the horses here a while and maybe see if Elwood can catch up?'

The pained expression on Ike's face as he turned back to him was answer enough.

'Paw says we keep on going past here and down the mountains on the other side to wherever the badlands are. That's what I mean to do. If you want to spend your time sittin' here waiting for him, you're on your own. Just remember there might be a whole lot more than Elwood coming. Maybe Dickson or a posse could be dogging our trail. You wanna wait for that, go 'head. We're gonna need all the guns we can get if either one catches up to us. That includes you, too. We have to stick together to save our own hides. The sooner you understand that the longer you'll live — and me and your brother too!'

The sun was disappearing behind tall

pines when the brothers rode down the single street of Fool's Gold. Even though the small, busy town was filled with rough and dirty looking men from all the mining activity, the Goss boys stood out because of their sullen faces, trail-worn horses and array of weapons they carried. Pistols stuck out of pants tops, all three had rifles cross slung on their backs and Ike had his shotgun slung in a scabbard on the side of his horse. It only took one glance to know these men were not prospectors or miners.

'We gonna try and stay overnight?' Emmett turned to Ike.

'I hate to slow down. We've done good so far, but these horses need a rest. Maybe we can take a little time to throw a blanket in timber at the far end of town out of sight. I ain't gonna pay for no hotel or cot house even if they have one here. We have ta be where we can see the main street and move fast if trouble shows up. Let's get on up there.'

Reaching a thick stand of pines, the three men got down. Ike insisted they leave the horses saddled in case of a fast exit. He had another order. 'One of us has to stay up and keep watch on town. Emmett, you're always worryin' about Elwood, so you take first watch, and don't go to sleep. You can wake Virgil up at midnight and he can take it until dawn.'

'What about you, Ike?' Virgil responded. 'Why ain't you takin' a watch?'

'Because I have ta think for you two and need some rest to keep our necks out of a noose. Spread them blankets out and let's get to it, and don't neither one of you go makin' no fire neither.'

Emmett pulled a blanket up over his shoulders, wrapping it around him, leaning back on a tree trunk. He glanced at his brothers laying with their rifles and pistols next to them in quick reach as they pulled thin blankets over themselves and hats down over their faces. He let out a long breath before turning his focus on the street a hundred yards away. Night was coming fast. As shadows ate up daylight, the windows of four saloons on the street lit with the glow of lamplight. Dark figures of evening drinkers and gamblers crossed the street hoping to change their luck. Emmett could hear occasional bursts of boisterous laughter from whiskey houses. His thoughts naturally turned to home, wondering what his mother and father were doing. He wished he could be there instead of out on the trail running for his life from something none of them was sure of. Ike's loud snoring broke his concentration. He looked over at his brothers. Virgil lay curled up in a ball, face hidden under a tattered hat. Ike's whiskered face was barely visible. Emmett thought his older brother must have ice water in his veins the way he let Elwood live or die, leaving him behind. Ike was a lot more like their father; cold, calculating, unforgiving. He pulled the blanket up higher around his neck as cold began creeping in.

Maybe the shivering would help him stay awake until midnight.

*   *   *

Ben Dickson rode steadily into that night without stopping to rest. He'd done this so many times before it was pure habit, closing in on men while they foolishly slept. Fool's Gold couldn't be more than another half day ahead. Maybe he'd find the Goss brothers there and finish off the chase in a quick showdown. The sooner he did, the faster he could get back to town, collect his fee, and pack up for home. These three were just a trio of back-alley back shooters looking for easy pickings. Facing his short-barrelled shotgun, they just might throw up their hands and give up without firing a shot. Or maybe not.

*   *   *

Hours later, Emmett pulled his pocket watch up close against his face trying to read the time. It looked like straight up twelve o'clock, but he couldn't be sure. Turning away from his sleeping brothers he struck a match, shielding its sudden flame. He was relieved to see it was time for his brother to take over and stand his watch.

'Virgil, wake up.' He shook him firmly. 'It's your turn.'

Virgil groaned sleepily, refusing to move.

'Come on. You've got to take your turn. I've done mine like Ike said.'

Virgil still refused to move. Emmett yanked the cover completely off him, repeating the demand. Virgil suddenly rolled up on his knees, wildly swinging fists pummeling Emmett, driving him on to his back while he was on top, continuing to throw punches. Ike sat up to the sudden commotion, trying to clear his head. Getting to his feet he grabbed both men by their long hair, slamming their heads together before yanking them apart.

'What in hell are you two idiots

doing! You want everyone in town to know we're out here? Virgil, you take your turn and I better not catch you fallin' back asleep, or I'll bust your head open. Emmett, you shut up and lay down. If I hear either one of you again before dawn, someone is gonna be bleedin'. Now shut up and be quiet!'

Emmett rolled up in his blanket wiping a bloody nose, while Virgil tried rubbing the sleep out of his eyes before sitting up against the tree for support. He focused on the street. The longer he stared, the more blurred his vision became. Half an hour later heavy eyelids closed and his head began to drop. He caught himself struggling to fight off the overpowering urge to sleep, rubbing his face with both hands. The easy tempo of Ike's renewed snoring only made the fight to stay awake even worse. Ten minutes later Virgil's head slowly dropped again. This time he did not wake up.

★ ★ ★

Dickson rode steadily until the first meagre slash of dawn painted the eastern sky, silhouetting tall pines above Fool's Gold. Reining to a halt he looked down on the sleepy little town. Only the fading glow of lamplight through windows could be seen. Store fronts were shuttered black. No figures moved on dirt sidewalks. No sound of voices drifted up from below. Dickson urged horse and packer down the narrow trail leading into town. His senses were suddenly heightened; he might find the brothers right here and finish off the whole chase without going further or wasting more valuable time. The Goss brothers had already given him enough trouble. He was anxious to end it.

6

Emerging from timber at the edge of town, the tall man pulled to a stop carefully studying the row of buildings and empty street. A single horse stood head down, tied in front of one all-night bar. If the brothers were here someplace it wasn't on this street. He urged horse and packer ahead until pulling to a stop in front of the bar. Before getting down he pulled the shotgun out of its scabbard, just to be sure there weren't any surprises waiting inside. The weight and heft of the big double barrel was always the best kind of life insurance. Edging to the door he looked inside. The only customer leaning at the bar was an old man talking to the counter man. Dickson stepped inside, quickly surveying the room and empty tables. The pair turned to his sudden footsteps.

'Mister, you don't need any shotgun to come in here,' the bartender exclaimed.

Dickson gave the room another long look before walking up to the bar. 'Either of you see three men come riding into town yesterday?'

'I don't pay much attention to who comes and goes. How about you, Harley?'

Harley Graves weaved slightly trying to maintain his balance, eyeing the tall man and his dark-barrelled shotgun up and down. For the moment, he did not answer.

'You have a hotel here in town?' Dickson asked.

'I wouldn't exactly call it a hotel. What we've got is a cot house. For two bits you can rent a cot for the night. That's about it,' the barman answered.

'Is it on this street?'

'No, it's behind Somerset's Dry Goods store, across the alley in back. You can't miss it once you get near. The smell will tell you when you're close. If you want to put that shotgun away you can buy a drink for all the free information I gave you.'

'I'm not drinking. I want to know if three riders came through here today.'

'Like I said, I don't keep track of strangers. And Harley here is only interested in another bottle of Old Stump Blower, so it's a waste of time asking him about anything. Ain't that right, Harley?'

Graves gazed at Dickson through a foggy, whiskey grin, waving his hand toward the front door. 'Three . . . men . . . they rode up . . . in the woods. I seen 'em.'

The barman smiled, shaking his head, glancing at Dickson. 'Listen Mister, Harley don't even know his own name when he's loaded like this. Don't pay him any mind. He just wants someone new to talk to, that's all.'

Dickson ignored the remark, stepping closer, putting a hand on the old man's shoulder for emphasis. 'Can you show me where they went?'

A dopey smile came over Harley's face, slowly nodding yes. Dickson grabbed him by the back of his belt, keeping him upright, crossing the room out the front door. Graves blinked, trying to focus his eyes. Lifting an arm he pointed toward a grove of trees at the far end of town. 'They . . . went in . . . there. Jus' like I . . . said.'

Dickson steered the old drunk to a bench outside the bar, sitting him down. 'You stay right here. Thanks for the information.'

'Did . . . I . . . do good?'

'You just might have.' He slipped a silver dollar in Harley's pocket.

⋆ ⋆ ⋆

Ike woke squinting into a thin streak of grey sky that was dawn. He rolled over, seeing Emmett still asleep a few feet away. Raising up on one elbow he saw Virgil, head down, sound asleep. Leaping to his feet, he began furiously slapping Virgil repeatedly across his face using his hat.

'You son of a — '

'Stop, Ike . . . I only fell asleep for a few minutes!' Virgil covered up with both hands, trying to ward off the strikes.

'I told you to stand your time in case someone was trailing us and you fall flat on your face, you damn fool!'

Emmett sat up to the sudden yelling as Ike continued cussing Virgil out. Rubbing the sleep out of his eyes he got to his feet trying to get Ike to stop. Doing so, his eyes focused down the street in town. He blinked, shaking his head, taking a longer look this time. A rider was coming down the street pulling a pack horse. He leaned forward, taking a longer look this time to be certain his eyes weren't playing tricks on him. Reaching over, he grabbed Ike by the shoulder.

'You better take a look at this. Look down there on the street. That could be trouble coming.'

Ike stopped berating Virgil long enough to follow Emmett's gaze. He squinted, shading his eyes with one hand, studying the approaching horseman. The tall man wore dark clothes and a wide-brimmed hat. He knew that figure. He'd seen him before the night they tried to kill Ben Dickson. It sent a sudden shock wave through him.

'Git your rifles. That has to be Dickson, for sure. Let 'em git closer to be sure we kill him this time!'

The three scrambled for long guns, returning where they had a clear view of the street, as Ike whispered orders. 'Not yet. Let 'em keep on comin'. Be steady before you pull that trigger. I'll say when.'

Dickson rode slowly forward, eyes searching the distant tree line Harley had pointed out. If no one else believed the old drunk, he did. He reined his horse to a stop halfway there for a better look.

'He's stoppin' Ike.' Virgil's voice was tinged with fear. 'We better shoot now!'

Before Ike could stop him, Virgil's rifle barked the first shot, forcing him and Emmett to quickly open up, too.

Bullets tore into Dickson's horse, the big animal rearing up, screaming in pain, tossing Dickson to the ground as rifle fire continued and the horse crashed to the ground, struggling in its dying throes. Dickson crawled up behind the animal for protection, yanking his shotgun out of its scabbard, as bullets thudded into the street around him sending up sudden geysers of dirt. He pulled his Colt, firing fast back at the flashes coming from the dark timber pocket.

'Let's get out of here!' Virgil yelled, getting to his feet.

'No, keep on firing. We gotta kill him right here!' Ike yelled back.

'Not me. I'm riding!' Virgil ran for the horses picketed behind them as Ike tried to stop him.

'Come back here you coward!' he screamed, but Virgil was already up in the saddle kicking his horse away.

'Let's ride too.' Emmett's voice mirrored his brother's, rising to his feet. 'We missed our chance. Let's not stay and let Dickson get any closer!'

Dickson saw the fleeting image of running horses behind a screen of timber, followed by fading hoof beats. He rose to his feet surveying his dead horse, running a hand over its warm body. It gave him another reason to even the score with the Goss brothers. The big animal had never failed him. It took a hail of their bullets to do so now. With the shooting ended, a handful of men exited the all-night bars, coming out on to the street wondering what all the sudden gunfire was about. Even Harley Graves, with the bartender steering him, came up the street. Dickson turned as the old man pushed through the circle of excited people.

'You saved my neck, old timer. If it wasn't for your warning, I'd be laying in the street right now instead of my horse. I owe you for that one.'

Harley flashed his slow motion grin, shaking a finger at the tall man. 'I toldja so. I seen 'em, just like I said.'

'That you did.' Dickson nodded,

turning to look at the other men around him with a request. 'Can I get some help getting my horse off the street? I need a couple of horses and ropes. I'll have to get my packer too. He ran off down the street.'

'What are you going to do now, stranger?' one man asked.

'I'm going to saddle up the packer and go after the men who just tried to kill me. They'll leave a trail a schoolboy could follow. I've been out of school a long time, but I still know how it's done.'

★　★　★

The Goss brothers rode like the devil himself was after them. Maybe Ben Dickson was exactly that. If Virgil was spooked before the shootout in town, he was more frantic now that it had failed and Dickson was still alive, coming after them. He continually surged his horse ahead of Ike, riding like a wild man, forcing the animal through thickets of dog hair timber, snapping off limbs and branches that could suddenly impale a man like a spear. Ike and Emmett kicked after him trying to slow him down until Ike finally found an opening where he could ride up alongside him, pulling his horse to a sudden stop.

'What are you tryin' to do, kill us? You get hold of yourself before I have to pull you out of that saddle and beat some sense into you. We're leavin' a back trail a blind man can follow. I'm takin' the lead and you stay behind me. If you don't I'll shoot your horse and put you afoot. You can face Dickson on your own. You understand me?'

Virgil's eyes bulged with fear. His mouth hung half open. Swallowing hard, he tried to get words out. 'He's coming and nothing is going to stop him. Not you, me or Emmett. That's twice we couldn't kill him. He ain't no normal man. Our only chance is to get as far away as we can, as fast as we can. That's all I'm trying to do.'

'Listen to me, you idiot. That's exactly what he wants you to think. He bleeds just like any other man. All we gotta do is get a bullet in him. He wants you to run wild so it's easy to follow us. Are you so dumb you can't see that? What we gotta do is think smart and move careful. That's what we're going to do and that means you, too. Settle down and start using your head before you get us all killed!'

The brothers rode steadily downhill for the next six days until thick timber ridges and high peaks began fading away behind them. The country ahead was lower, more open, changing rapidly. When they broke out of the last timber and reined to a halt, the scene that met their eyes stunned all three to silence. As far as the eye could see the land was a jumbled mass of wildly eroded buttes, canyons and treeless flats, grey and foreboding. Ike took in a deep breath before speaking.

'I ain't never seen any country looked like this. I guess Paw knew what he was talking about. Even a rattlesnake would starve to death out there. It must be the badlands.'

'Then how are we supposed to make it?' Emmett's worried whisper questioned.

'I ain't sure right now. But if Dickson is still coming on he'll have to face this too. And we got a better chance of killing him out there than back in the mountains.'

The brothers rode cautiously out into the grotesquely twisted land, staying on narrow trails with pebbly bottoms. Ike turned in the saddle looking back to see if the horses were leaving hoof prints on the hard-packed ground. They were barely visible. One brief rain would easily wash them away. In the myriad twists and turns it took to stay in the bottoms, it grew more difficult as the day wore on to know which way they were actually riding. The sun was a steel grey disk behind cloudy skies with enough light for them to guess they were moving east, farther out into the badlands. Four more days of winding in and out of crumbling canyons found the brothers entering an unusual series of low, flat-topped mesas situated in a semi-circle. Ike pulled to a halt studying the strange formations, instantly realizing its potential as a perfect spot for ambushing Dickson. A leering smile began creasing his whiskered face, as his brothers rode up on both sides of him.

'You see what I see?' Ike asked, looking from Virgil to Emmett.

'Ah, what?' Emmett questioned, swivelling his head.

'Open your eyes, both of you. This is the perfect place to wait for Dickson. When he comes riding in here we can take him with rifles from three different angles. He'll be a dead man for sure, not like back in Peralta.'

'What if he don't come this way, then what?' Virgil's voice was tight as a fiddle string.

'He'll come. If you two paid any attention to what's going on around you instead of acting like scared rabbits, you'd know it ain't rained.'

'What's that got to do with it?' Emmett asked.

'He can follow our tracks, that's what. He'll be here all right. And this time when we're done he'll stay dead. We're done runnin'. Now it's time for killin'!'

The three spent the rest of that day exploring the half circle of low buttes, pockets and narrow ravines fronting the trail leading in. Ike chose to set up camp in a shallow cave that could not be seen from the trail, picketing the horses out of sight. After unloading what few supplies they had left, all three dug shallow pits big enough to lay in with a berm on one edge to rest rifles over. The three spots, in the form of a 'U', were only thirty feet apart end to end. Ike reasoned all three could reach their position quickly out of sight. The narrow trail they expected Dickson to ride in on was barely one hundred yards away.

The brothers had a heated discussion

on whether or not they should stand a night watch. Ike said he wasn't for it because he didn't believe even Dickson could track them in the dark over hard ground. Emmett wasn't so sure. He argued the tall man might keep riding at least during part of the night to gain ground on them, just like he did reaching Fool's Gold. Virgil, nervous as always, volunteered to stand the first watch and not take any chances. Ike was quick to remind him how he fell asleep back in town, nearly letting Dickson catch all of them sleeping.

'This is different,' Virgil countered. 'I won't do that again no matter what. I promise I won't. I want to kill him just as bad as you two do and ride back home where we belong, instead of hiding out in this godforsaken land. This place ain't fit for no human being to be in. There's no game or much of anything else.'

Ike and Emmett stared back at their brother. Both were thinking exactly the same thing without saying so out loud.

Neither trusted him, no matter how much he tried to make them believe him. Both would have been stunned to know Ben Dickson was doing exactly what their brother just said. When he pulled to a stop getting his first look at the badlands, Dickson knew tracking the Goss brothers had suddenly changed, and not for the better. There would be no more easy tracking over soft ground through broken brush and tall willow thickets. These bare, treeless buttes, crumbling cliffs and the stark grey landscape made following the three harder and much more dangerous. In this kind of broken land the brothers could be hiding anyplace, watching and waiting to ambush him. Dickson leaned back in the saddle as his mind wrestled with the new circumstances. He also considered that his original timetable of collecting his blood money from Rolo Mackenzie and Edward Chambers had changed too. He urged his horse down toward the first narrow canyon ahead where tracks said the trio had also entered. As canyon walls rose around him he leaned lower in the saddle, barely able to make out the faintest hoof prints etched in flinty ground leading away. It was enough to follow, at least for now. That's all that mattered.

The man hunter knew something else even more important learned from tracking other men that had run for weeks and long distances. Almost always they slowed down after five or six days, thinking they'd outridden a prison sentence or a hangman's noose.

The Goss brothers would be no different. They came from a close-knit family that stuck together and acted together on whatever they did. Here in the badlands they were far from home without their domineering father telling them what to do and when to do it. They were in strangely twisted country they'd never seen before and that was another big disadvantage for them. It would make them prone to crucial mistakes, arguing with each other about where to go, when to stop, and what to do next. Every day Dickson didn't show up could give them false hope he'd either given up and turned back, or got lost himself in this jigsaw puzzle land. As more days followed they might even decide it was safe to start back for home. All these possibilities worked in Dickson's favour and he well knew it. His decision was to ride well into the night, at least for the next three or four days. That way he could close distance on the brothers as they slept.

An October Hunter's Moon lit the ground casting ghostly shadows around Dickson as he sat easy in the saddle, letting his horse set its own pace. There was no rush or reason to move faster. He'd gained valuable ground all that week and the slow pace allowed him time to search ahead each night for the faint glow of a dying camp fire. The full moon in a velvet black sky stood out like a bright beacon. Sometime after midnight Dickson pulled a pocket watch from his vest, lifting it closer. Moon glow lit its white enamelled face outlining black numbers. 1:47. He decided to stop for the night and bed down for a few hours, saddling up again at first light.

* * *

Dawn, when it came, blew in on a bitter wind forcing Virgil to roll over, shivering under his thin wool blanket. He struggled to his feet, wrapping the blanket over his shoulders, pulling his beat up hat down around his ears.

'Ike, we're out of water for coffee.' He tried rousing his brother, still down. 'Forget coffee. We ain't got that much left anyway. What we need is water. Our bags are nearly empty. Go back to that mud hole we saw ridin' in and fill up all three water bags. Emmett and I will try to git a fire goin' to warm up. We're gonna need more wood too, but there ain't much around here. If you find some, grab it up.'

Virgil stared back wide-eyed. The last thing he wanted to do was leave camp alone. The fear that Dickson might show up was more than he could take. The thought of it haunted him constantly. 'I . . . can't go back. One of you will have to ride with me.'

'What'ya mean you can't? Dickson might have already gave up and turned back by now. It's been weeks since we seen him. Even if he didn't he'd still be miles away. Get a grip on yourself and get going. There ain't no ghosts out here 'cept the ones in your head!'

Virgil grudgingly saddled his horse, looping the three water bags over the saddle horn. He swung up holding a rifle in one hand. Looking back he saw Ike and Emmett still wrapped in blankets. Anger rose in him, being forced out alone. The moment his horse reached stony flats down from camp, he felt the knot in his stomach beginning to grow. For the entire mile ride to water, his head constantly swivelled side to side, searching as dawn began brightening the land around him.

The water hole was little more than a muddy crease bubbling to the surface.

Virgil slid the rifle back in its scabbard. Getting down he lifted the water bags free, kneeling to dip the first bag into the shallow, silted pool. The slow gurgle as it tried to fill immediately frustrated him. He wanted to get the job done and get back to the safety of camp fast. Minutes ticked by agonizingly slowly until the first canvas bag bulged full. Capping it he pushed the second one in, glancing back over his shoulder to be sure he was alone. Nothing stirred. No bird sang. The land around him seemed dead as the waning moon.

Finishing the second bag he plunged a third into the water, watching bubbles slowly burping to the surface as it filled. Finally finished he got to his feet, twisting the cap on, turning toward his horse. When he looked up he suddenly saw the dark figure of Ben Dickson, standing like a ghost thirty feet away, staring at him with a shotgun levelled in his hands. Virgil's eyes bulged in wild fear. His mouth fell open unable to yell and his breath came in short gasps as his body became paralyzed.

'Drop the water bags, and unbuckle your gun belt, left handed. Don't make me kill you right here,' Dickson ordered in an even voice. 'They'll be a hangman waiting for you and your brothers back in Peralta. Where are they?'

Virgil still clung to the water bag, unable to unclench his hands. His arms slowly fell to his sides until he was able to drop the heavy bag at his feet with a soggy thud. He swallowed hard, trying to find his voice as his mind raced. How had Dickson suddenly appeared from out of nowhere without a sound? His confusion matched his fear.

'Drop that gun belt. I won't tell you again.'

Virgil swallowed hard, biting his lip. He took in a deep breath trying to unlock his frozen body, finally getting out a few words.

'I . . . ain't going back . . . nowhere.' He amazed himself at his own refusal.

'You're going back either in hand-cuffs, or roped over your horse like a sack of wheat. The choice is yours. Make up your mind and do it right now.'

Virgil's hand just touched the cold leather of the holster on his side. All he had to do was take that one chance he could pull it fast enough to fire. He stood at the edge of eternity. Which way to go? He stabbed at the six gun, never clearing the holster before the roar of Dickson's shotgun made the choice for him. It would be eternity.

7

Ike jumped straight up out of his blanket, wild-eyed at the sudden report of a distant shotgun. Emmett shucked his blankets seconds later, getting to his feet too.

'Virgil didn't take no shotgun with him.' Ike eyed his brother. 'Let's start packin' up this gear right now. If he don't show back here in ten minutes, we're leavin' without him!'

'Wait, Ike. We can't just ride off without knowing if Virgil's alive or not. We've got to go back and find him. Maybe he needs help?'

'You wanna ride back, go ahead. But don't look for me. I'm makin' tracks out of here now.'

'Hold on a minute. Maybe he got a shot at some game? We need something to eat, that's for sure. It don't have to be any trouble.'

'Emmett, use your head. That was no rifle shot. It was a shotgun. Virgil wasn't packin' any shotgun. Now stop yer jawin' and help me pick up our gear. We gotta get out of here. I don't know if it was Dickson or someone else, but I ain't stayin' to find out!'

* * *

Dickson didn't get the answer he wanted about where Virgil's brothers were, but he knew they couldn't be very far. He had to move fast because it was just as likely they'd heard his shot. He quickly roped up Virgil's body with his own lariat, grunting to lift the dead weight on to his horse, tying it over the saddle. Mounting up he pulled the horse behind, following tracks in the direction from which Virgil had come. It wasn't the first time Ben Dickson had hauled his victims roped over their saddles behind him. He took some kind of morbid pride as a man-killer bringing in bodies for all to see, wonder and gawk at. It cemented his reputation with powerful men of money who heard of his unbelievable exploits and were willing to pay and pay big for his brand of six-gun justice, having their 'problems' removed too, while keeping their hands and reputation clean of bloody murder charges.

The moment Dickson reached the stony amphitheatre, he instantly reined to a halt. One quick look was all he needed to realize this was a perfect place for an ambush. Reining his horse back into the cover of canyon walls, he dismounted, pulling his shotgun out of its scabbard, before starting carefully around the semi-circle behind tall boulders. At the far end of the semi-circle he eased through a narrow gap, shotgun held belt-buckle high with both hammers pulled back. Fresh boot tracks led to the abandoned cave campsite. Virgil's blanket lay in one spot, a few extra cartridges atop it. Ashes in the shallow fire pit were still smoking. The brothers had fled even before the chance to warm up around a morning fire. Yards behind the shallow cave he found where the horses had been tethered. Their tracks led away due east farther into the land of crumbling cliffs and eroded buttes. Dickson straightened up, lowering the shotgun. He'd only missed the pair by minutes, but he consoled himself that at least he'd already killed two of the Goss brothers. That only left two more to finish the job. Back at the horses, he tied Virgil's blanket over his body before saddling up, picking up Ike and Emmett's tracks at the far end of the stone circle. They would be even more dangerous now knowing he was so close behind. They were more likely to make mistakes trying to either outrun him or lure him into another ambush. If those failed they might even stop running and wait to face him for a showdown with the odds still on their side. He'd been lucky to catch Virgil like he did. He couldn't expect that kind of luck to happen twice. Especially not with two men instead of one.

★ ★ ★

Far ahead in the puzzle of endless canyons, Ike was in the lead whipping his horse down one twisting trail after another, not knowing where any of them led. Emmett clung to his saddle spurring his horse right behind him, yelling at him to slow down, to no avail. Their frantic running left a trail easy to follow even on hard ground. Dickson followed it all that day until late afternoon when a milky sun began its downward arc toward evening.

Ike, on another wild ride, suddenly found himself riding full out around a corner into a dead-end box canyon. Rearing back on the reins he hauled his horse to a skidding stop, but not before Emmett rode in right behind him at full gallop, trying to stop. His horse slipped on the pebbly trail, its hind leg falling into a narrow crevice. The pistol crack of breaking bones reverberated off canyon walls as the horse went down, Emmett thrown completely over its head smashing face-first on to the ground. The injured horse screamed in pain, struggling to right itself only to fall back again. Emmett staggered to unsteady feet, cut and bleeding from the sudden impact, trying to clear his head. Ike was off his horse wildly waving his hands, already confronting him.

'Now you went and done it. You're afoot, you damn fool!'

'You stopped so fast I couldn't help it. If you hadn't been riding like a wild man — '

'I'm ridin' to keep us from ending up like Virgil likely did. Are you so stupid you can't figure that out?'

'Well . . . we'll have to ride double now. I can figure that out.'

'Ridin' double only means Dickson can catch up to us faster. I ought to let you walk out of here and see how far you git!'

Emmett stood staring back at his brother, wondering if he was crazy enough to really leave him. 'You said we have to stick together, didn't you? We better do that now and get out of here and stop yelling about it.'

Ike's face turned red with rage. He started to cuss Emmett out again, suddenly pulling his gun. Emmett threw up both hands over his face until the pistol shot into his horse's head ended the animal's pitiful squealing.

'Git your stuff off that horse and climb on in back. Then shut up. I don't want to hear any more of your advice!'

* * *

Dickson pulled his horse to a stop, listening intently. He thought he'd heard the distant 'thud' of a pistol shot. He sat stock still, but only silence met his ears. It had to come from the brothers someplace ahead — but why? They knew he was trailing them. It didn't make any sense unless something unforeseen had happened. Surely there was no one else in this miserable land. He urged his horse forward, following easy tracks etched in gravelly ground.

Ike kept his horse moving steadily through-out that day but the worry furrowing his whiskered face only grew worse. He knew what riding double meant. Everything seemed to be turning against him. Virgil was dead and likely Elwood too. Now Emmett's horse was done in. His own horse wasn't going to last long carrying double either. His mind spun with the odds against them. Sooner or later Dickson would catch up to them — probably sooner. He had to do something drastic, something unexpected, and do it quick. For the first time in his chaotic life, Ike Goss felt real fear of another man who wasn't his maniacal father. He began wondering if Virgil wasn't right after all when he'd said Ben Dickson was a devil in man's clothing. Maybe he was.

That evening after they'd stopped for the day in a small side canyon, Ike sat up late wrapped in a blanket to protect him against dropping temperatures in their fire-less campsite. Emmett lay rolled up in his blanket, mumbling and twitching through troubled sleep full of reccurring nightmares. Ike stared down at him, wondering just how much he could depend on his brother when it came down to a face to face gunfight with Dickson. He wasn't sure anymore, adding to his other worries. Slowly, desperately, he began to form a wild plan that might save them both. The more he thought it over, the more convinced he became it was their best chance to rid themselves of the relentless lawman. He rocked back and forth, eyes closed, visualizing exactly how it could work.

Instead of continuing to run he'd let Dickson catch up to them on purpose. This time he'd ride into an ambush he couldn't slip out of. Emmett would be the bait, whether he liked it or not. Dickson would find Emmett's horse and know they had to ride double. He'd catch up to them twice as fast because of it. When he did Ike would put his brother afoot, out in the open, when they found the perfect spot for the ambush. When Dickson came on fast to take Emmett down, he'd rise from cover close by and finish him off with his rifle. It was the perfect plan. It had to work. It was their last chance to escape.

Emmett shivered awake at dawn, peering out from under his blanket to find Ike sitting up, eyes closed but not asleep.

'Ike . . . you awake?'

Ike slowly opened bloodshot eyes. 'Yeah, I'm awake. Have been most of the night.'

'We better saddle up and get going? Dickson sure will and we need to make tracks.'

'No, that's what I've been thinkin' about all night. We ain't gonna run no more.'

Emmett quickly sat up, blinking in confusion. 'What are you talking about?'

'I mean we're done tryin' to outrun him ridin' double. We're gonna let him think he's got us. We're gonna let him catch up to us. Then when he closes in, I'll kill him.'

Emmett threw off the blanket. 'We already tried that back in Fool's Gold. It didn't work, remember? Why even think about trying it again? That makes no sense, Ike.'

'This time it's gonna be different. You're the bait that brings him in real close. When you do, I'll drop the hammer on 'em.'

'What do you mean, I'm the bait?'

'Shut up and listen to me. I'll explain it to you real slow so you can't mess up.'

Ike went over his risky plan while Emmett's eyes grew wider with each sentence. When he finished Emmett was already on his feet, vigorously shaking his head.

'I'm not going to go and get myself killed like that. It's a crazy idea and you're crazy for even thinking it up.'

'You're gonna do it all right or I'll saddle up right now and leave you afoot. Dickson will run you down even faster. Take your pick, Emmett!'

'That isn't any kind of choice, for God's sake.'

'Yeah it is. You and me are ridin' out of here just far enough to find a place on open ground where I can finish him off. When we do, we'll wait for him to show up.'

Emmett's heart pounded in his chest with fear of what could happen to him. Ike's insane plan made no sense, but he wouldn't listen. He started to protest again but Ike had already turned away, heading for his horse to mount up.

★   ★   ★

Later that same day Dickson followed horse tracks into the narrow side canyon, its steep walls closing in on him the further he went. He pulled the shotgun from its scabbard resting the stock on his leg, barrels up, one hand gripping the fore stock. At short range the scattergun cut a wider swath of death than his pistol. Near the end he rounded a tight right turn to see black-winged vultures suddenly scramble into the air with a flurry of wings, and the reason why; Emmett's dead horse. Reining to a stop he eased out of the saddle. Closely hugging one wall, eyes scanning stony heights above for any sign of ambush, he stepped closer to the dead animal. The birds had just begun opening it up with their razor-sharp beaks. The scattering of discarded clothes plus a cloth-wrapped package of hard tack made it clear the brothers left in a hurry and had to be riding double. He leaned closer, studying the animal. It was still fresh. That meant it could not be more than a day old or possibly even killed earlier that morning. A small smile lit his unshaven face. He was certain now he'd catch up to Ike and Emmett possibly later today or early tomorrow. The long ride over one hundred miles and weeks of trailing would finally be over. He mounted up pulling Virgil's horse behind him with his roped body blanket-wrapped, stiff as a board, the odour of death growing stronger each day. It didn't bother Ben Dickson. He was used to the smell of death. He'd made a good living off of it. He was just as certain when he caught up to Ike and Emmett, he'd be pulling three horses behind with their load of dead men too.

★   ★   ★

To the west far over the mountains, the afternoon sun was fading over Peralta country. Vernal Goss sat in his chair on the porch staring out at timber-clad mountains surrounding his broken down ranch house. His tired face lined with deep creases only made him look even older than he was. He lifted a bony hand to his face, stroking a scraggly beard as his thoughts turned to his boys once again. If only he could stand and saddle a horse, he'd be with them right now, and Ben Dickson would be a dead man. He'd seen he needed killing the first time he'd ridden out to his ranch demanding answers, acting high and mighty. He might wear a tin star, but that meant nothing to Goss. He hated to admit it to himself but wondered if his boys had the grit to do it as easily as he would. He told them when they left it would take time for things to cool down. Even though it had only been just over a month, he was anxious to hear something from at least one of them.

Hattie pushed through a squeaky screen door stepping out on to the porch, coming up behind her husband. She hesitated a moment before resting her hands on Vernal's stooped shoulders, in a rare show of emotion. Even the misery and daily demands he made on her could not hide that deep down she knew he was as worried about the boys as she was. Vernal felt her tiny hands but did not react until she leaned closer, whispering in his ear.

'I've been thinking about the boys. I know they haven't been gone all that long, but I still can't help it. Do you think they're all right, Vernal?'

Goss tried to straighten up, taking in a gravelly breath. 'If they did what I told 'em to and stayed together, they'll be all right. If they get scatterbrained, then I don't know. Dickson's no ghost. He's a man like any other man. He bleeds when someone gets a bullet in him. He dies just like anyone else. All they gotta do is get that bullet in him. I shoulda done it myself when he rode out here that first time. If I ever get another chance, I won't make that mistake twice. I'll give him both barrels right quick!'

★   ★   ★

In the mine office in Peralta, Rolo Mackenzie pushed back his chair from the desk, closing his eyes as he massaged the back of his neck, letting out a long sigh of relief. The endless paperwork, columns of numbers on the mine operation and map study, had worn him out. His partner, Edward Chambers, turned in his swivel chair, studying Rolo a moment.

'Let's take a break. We both could use one.' He got to his feet heading for a small wood stove in the middle of the room, stuffing in fresh wood. 'Winter must be just around the corner. It's getting cold even in the afternoon now.'

Rolo got to his feet, walking to the window facing the street. People passed by up and down the boardwalk as a large wagon pulled by a team of horses loaded with supplies for the dry goods store rattled by. A pair of horsemen passed in the opposite direction. It all seemed so normal, just another day in the growing town of Peralta. But Rolo knew it was not. Ben Dickson had left well over a month ago after the Goss brothers, and no one had heard a single word about him since. That thought never left Rolo's mind. He'd mentioned it to Edward more than once. This time his partner stood watching him, reading his mind.

'Still thinking about Dickson?'

He turned from the window, looking back at Chambers. 'Yeah, I guess I am. I try not to but I can't help it. One man against four? What kind of odds is that for any man to go up against and come out on top?'

'Dickson is not just any man. We both knew his reputation when we hired him. This is his specialty.'

'I've been thinking what if the brothers kill him instead? They might come back here and take it out on us. Did you ever think of that? They're just as crazy as their father, you know.'

Chambers didn't answer immediately, thinking the question over. When he did he startled Rolo. 'Well, if you're that worried about it happening, we might want to start carrying pistols ourselves.'

'I'm no gunman, Edward. I'd just as likely shoot myself in the foot.'

'Then let's wait until Dickson gets back, if he gets back, and stop worrying about it. For now I say let's close up the office early and take a break. We've got another load of ore heading down for Marysville, and I want to talk to the driver before he pulls out.'

Rolo looked at his partner, nodding in agreement, but he couldn't get the fate of Ben Dickson off his mind.

8

The sun rose the following morning, quickly losing itself behind the grey clouds scuttling by, carrying the scent of autumn in the air. The Goss brothers spent most of that morning looking back over their shoulders when Ike wasn't searching for a spot to set up his plan to ambush Dickson. Twisted canyons ran in every direction until near noon when they rode into the first piece of open ground they'd found. Ike immediately reined to a halt eyeing the area carefully. He pulled the horse in a slow circle studying every foot of it. It looked like a dry pan that held shallow water once winter rains came. Flat and open, it was bordered by large boulders where rocky buttes came down to meet it. The pan itself was shaped in an oval nearly one hundred yards at its longest point.

'This is it,' Ike exclaimed with a sinister smile. 'I could shoot the buttons off Dickson's shirt, this close. All you'll have to do is climb up top and keep your eyes open. When you see him ride in git your tail back down here out right out in the middle of this flat. He'll think he's caught you cold on foot. That's when I'll kill 'em.'

'Can't I at least be in the saddle? He might try to shoot me on sight!'

'No, he won't. He'll be lookin' for me. While you make up a story, he'll be dead before you finish. We're gonna turn around and ride right out this country soon as I kill 'em. What's left of Dickson, the buzzards can pick clean.'

While Emmett laboriously climbed the gravelly butte high enough to see back down the narrow trail leading in, Ike got comfortable behind boulders, resting his rifle over a higher one. To make the set-up even better, he took off his heavy jacket, folding it, resting the rifle over it for padding. When he snuggled in behind the rifle looking through the buckhorn sights, it was steady as a rock. His plan to actually let Dickson catch up to them when he thought he was still trying to run them down was pure genius. He knew Vernal, back home, would be proud of his scheming exactly like he'd done all his life. He turned from his rocky seat, looking up for Emmett.

'Hey, git yourself behind something taller. You're out in the open too much!'

Emmett moved a few feet until partly hidden. 'That's better. You stay right there and keep your eyes open. No tellin' when he might show up.'

Emmett crouched down at an uncomfortable angle, afraid to move as Ike might start yelling again. He could see the flat running away to the trail leading in, until it was lost farther back on a turn. He wondered how long he'd have to stay up here before scrambling back down out into the flat without being seen. Ike's wild plan to use him as bait still scared him stiff. What if something went wrong? What if Dickson opened fire the moment he saw him? What if Dickson never showed up at all? He and his brother could abandon the whole ambush idea and leave the badlands, riding for home.

Home. The very thought of even having to put up with Vernal seemed a dream a million miles away. How he wished he could see his mother again, smell the cooking pot boiling away on the wood stove, hug her frail body close to him again. He wished he'd never taken part in the robbery and killing of John Standard. He was no real gunman, no cold-blooded killer. It was Vernal who insisted on the robbery. And look what it had gotten all of them. Virgil and Elwood were dead while he and Ike were fighting for their lives trying to outsmart a real man killer. It was his father's fault for all this, not his or Ike's.

He stopped daydreaming, rubbing the fear out of his eyes. Straightening up he looked down on Ike sitting patiently, staring at the entrance to the flat. If anyone could kill Dickson, Ike could. He had the same kind of vicious attitude their father did. First born and oldest, Vernal had pounded his bitter psychology of life into him, beginning before he could even walk or speak one word. Those lessons took and took hard with Ike. His aggressive, swarthy attitude developed early and only grew worse as he grew older. And yet Ike was his best chance to kill Dickson and get them out of here for home. Emmett leaned back closing his eyes a moment, thinking all this over. It was so confusing. He needed rest and time to try making some sense of it.

'You keepin' your eyes open up there?' Ike's harsh bark broke his concentration.

'Yeah, I am. I just took a little break.'

'Don't be takin' no break. You stay sharp. We've gotta see Dickson before he does us. Then git yourself down here and do what I told ya!'

Emmett waved back. He tried studying the trail again, squinting until his eyes grew gritty. An hour passed and a second even slower. Nothing stirred. No bird winged across sullen skies. Monotony turned to boredom. Boredom turned to the overpowering urge to close his eyes and rest, even for only a few moments. He tried fighting it off, vigorously rubbing his whiskered face with both hands. It didn't work. Heavy eyelids grew heavier. Emmett closed his eyes, resting his head on both arms. He promised himself he'd only rest a few seconds. It felt so good, so relieving. His breathing began to slow as mind and body gave in and tension drained away. Ten seconds later he surrendered to the sleep he'd fought so hard to resist.

Ike fidgeted in his seat at the miserably slow passage of time and inaction. He constantly twisted, looking up for his brother, wondering why he couldn't see him. He couldn't trust Emmett to do anything right without watching him like a hawk. Before getting to his feet he surveyed the trail leading into the pan one more time, just to be sure. Taking several steps away he tried getting a different angle on the rocky slope above. He still could not see his brother. His frustration built until he dared take the chance to call up. Cupping both hands around his whiskered mouth he tried calling in a hoarse, deep-throated whisper. 'Emmett — Emmett, you up there?' After waiting a few moments with no response he tried again, louder this time. 'Emmett, damnit, answer me!'

Up in his stony bed, Emmett opened his eyes realizing he'd fallen asleep. Ike's gravelly voice spurred him into action, pulling himself up, rubbing the sleep out of his eyes. He heard Ike call again, even more demanding.

'I'm here.' He struggled to his knees, waving down. 'I was just . . . resting for a few minutes.'

'Don't you go resting nothin'. You stay sharp, you hear? We still got a couple more hours of daylight left. Dickson could show up any time!'

Ike went back to his rocky seat,

mumbling to himself while Emmett tried to clear his head, focusing again on the trail. As he settled down the same questions came back to haunt him again. What would happen if Dickson only showed up after dark? Would Ike even be able to see him to make a killing shot? Would he still have to go out in the middle of the flat and show himself like they'd planned earlier? Suddenly everything became more perplexing and muddled. He tried pushing disturbing thoughts aside, concentrating on the entrance trail.

That remaining afternoon passed excruciatingly slow until light began to fade. Both brothers struggled to stay alert, but when Dickson didn't show it became harder to stay on edge. Even Ike grew weary enough to get up, walking in small circles trying to keep himself ready. Above, in his rocky hide, Emmett vigorously rubbed his neck and massaged aching shoulders. He was tempted to abandon his perch and start down the gravelly slope. In another few minutes he'd have no choice. For the final time he squinted at the trail entrance. At first he wasn't sure tired eyes weren't playing tricks on him. He leaned closer as sundown shades of grey dimmed the land toward evening. The tiny figure of horse and rider seemed to fill the trail shadows. His heart jumped with alarm. He pulled himself up on both knees, concentrating harder. Now he could actually make out the outline of a man in the saddle dressed in dark clothes. It had to be Dickson, at last! Emmett rose to his feet. He wanted to shout down a warning to Ike, but stopped himself. Instead he began scrambling down the steep slope, stumbling and skidding as cascading rocks bounced noisily ahead of him until he reached the bottom. Ike was already on his feet cussing him out for making a racket, but Emmett's breathless warning stopped him.

'He's coming — Dickson's coming down the trail right now. I saw him for sure. He'll be here any minute!'

'I don't see nothin'. Are you sure?'

'I tell you I saw him from up there.' He flung an arm over his shoulder. 'Do I still have to go out in the flat? He might not even be able to see me by now.'

'We got no choice. You gotta do it. Run out there and remember, try to keep him talking long enough for me to git a bullet in him. That's all it's gonna take. Now move!'

The tall man rode down the walled trail, pulling Virgil's horse and body behind him as evening shadows cloaked the badlands further. Ahead he could see open ground for the first time that day. He quickly became cautious. He knew the brothers couldn't be far ahead. He'd made good time since finding Emmett's dead horse. The closer he got to the open pan, the more he realized what a large area it was and perfect for an ambush. Reaching the entrance he reined to a stop at its edge. Suddenly he saw Emmett halfway across out in the open, running wildly for the far end. Impulsively, he dropped the halter rope, spurring his horse after him on a ground-eating gallop, pulling his six-gun. Emmett looked back over his shoulder. Horse and rider were catching up fast. He stopped running, turning back, throwing up his hands and screaming for mercy.

'Don't shoot — I'm done in!' His eyes bulged with fear.

Dickson was off his horse levelling his pistol, stepping closer. 'Where's your brother? Answer me right now or you're a dead man!'

'He — he left me and rode out on his own. Said we couldn't ride double any more. Honest, that's the truth. I'm alone. You have to believe me!'

In the rocky hide fifty yards away, Ike slid the rifle out over his coat pulling it solid against his shoulder, centering the buckhorn sights on Dickson's tall image shrouded in evening gloom. His finger tightened on the trigger until the rifle exploded in sudden thunder, spinning Dickson to the ground with the white-hot whiplash of a bullet hit. Emmett jumped back, grabbing for his pistol, trying to finish Dickson off as he rolled on to his back firing two fast shots straight up, killing Emmett instantly. Ike saw his brother go down in a heap. Leaping from his hide he ran at Dickson, firing his rifle from the hip as fast as he could work the lever action. His wild shots tore into Emmett's dead body as Dickson pulled himself up against Emmett for a shield. Halfway across open ground, Dickson raised up firing two more shots, sending Ike crashing to the ground, bullet hits in both his legs, the rifle flying from his hands. Slowly, painfully, Dickson forced himself to his feet, advancing on Ike one staggering step at a time until standing over him, aiming his six-gun straight down in his face.

'Do it,' Ike growled. 'I ain't afraid to die, you bastard!'

'No, I won't kill you here. That's too easy. I'm taking you back to Peralta, so they can hang you in front of a Sunday crowd, watching you snap and kick while your face turns blue and your tongue sticks out. I've waited a long time to catch up to you. I can wait a little longer to see if you're afraid to die or not.'

Dickson reached down, yanking Ike's pistol from its holster. His face contorted in pain, defiantly glaring up at him. 'You think you're gonna get me back to Peralta? I can't even walk with my legs shot to pieces. And you're bleedin' out too. We ain't goin' anywhere, law dog. We'll both likely die right here in the badlands, and I'll watch you go first!'

Dickson stepped back opening his heavy coat, slipping Ike's pistol under his gun-belt. For the first time he looked down at his shirt, soaked red with blood. Carefully unbuttoning it he pulled it open, seeing a red gash across his chest where Ike's bullet had cut through clothes and skin but not penetrated into muscle and bone. He pulled the back of his hand across his mouth wiping away the sweat of pain and shock. Another inch deeper and he'd have been a dead man. Looking down at Ike, he made a vow he meant to keep.

'You're going back to Peralta all right even if I have to rope you in your saddle instead of over it. I don't care if your legs rot off before we get there either.'

Ike's eyes were filled with pure hate as he struggled to pull himself up on one elbow. He took in a faltering breath, staring up at Dickson. 'We ain't in Peralta yet. I say you'll never git me there . . . alive. Wanna bet on it?'

* * *

A tiny evening fire flickered in a surround of rocks as the lawman stripped to the waist, beginning to doctor himself. From his saddle-bags he'd retrieved a small kit of bandages and several flat tins containing different coloured powders. He gingerly patted the white powder across his chest, grimacing with pain at its fiery touch. Ike lay watching him propped up against a boulder, his hands cuffed behind his back. When Dickson finished he ripped his undershirt into narrow strips for makeshift bandages, wrapping them around his chest tying them off. Very carefully he slipped his shirt back on while looking over at Goss.

'You better pull them pants down and try doctoring yourself with this.' He tossed the white powder can to him. 'I don't want you to die of gangrene before I get you to town.'

'Are your ears stuffed? I told you already I ain't going back, and I ain't using that stuff either. I wanna know what's that roped on Virgil's horse?'

'It's your brother. Elwood's dead too. He's laying halfway back to Peralta. I'll pick him up when we get there.'

Ike's mouth twisted in revulsion and rage. Suddenly he tried lunging at Dickson, unable to reach him because of useless legs. 'You call me an animal, while you drag around bodies like they're somethin' to be proud of? Someone needs to kill you real quick before you can do it again. That badge don't make you no man. All it does is give you license to slaughter people and hide behind it. I'm gonna live long enough to watch you die real slow one way or the other!'

'If you try giving me any more trouble, I'll hog tie you once we start back so every time you move you'll choke yourself. You better get used to a rope around your neck. I'm going to see to it you'll be wearing one real soon.'

Two men wounded by each other sat opposite a small fire until it finally burned down to a pool of glowing red coals. Dickson propped himself up against his saddle, while Ike lay on his side glaring back. Neither spoke a single word for hours as a deathly game began playing itself out. It was a simple game both men knew had only one ending. Life or death? Who could outlast the other and not give in to sleep. If Dickson couldn't stay awake, Ike would drag himself over wrapping his manacled hands under his throat, choking him to death. He didn't need two good legs to do that. Ike already knew he had the edge. The lawman would have to stay awake watching him, while he could catch a few hours of much-needed sleep. Dickson could not.

The tall man leaned back, trying to forget the searing pain burning across his chest, concentrating instead on what the Goss brothers had already cost him in time, money and now physical pain that could become bad enough to disable him if things got worse. No other man or group of men had ever given him more trouble and misery. He was more determined than ever to make the last of the brothers pay for all of it in every way possible. If Ike died on the trail, so be it. At least he wouldn't always have to be on guard day and night to be sure he didn't get jumped. What he wanted most of all was to parade Ike down the main street in Peralta, pulling his dead brothers behind him, waiting for the public hanging that would end it all. He could collect his money, get some decent rest healing up, before starting for back home, to Arizona.

The strange procession that rode out of the badlands next morning was a macabre scene. Dickson put Ike in the lead, hands still cuffed behind his back, with Emmett and Virgil's bodies roped over their horses, tied in tandem behind him. Dickson rode last where he could keep an eye on Ike and his deadly cargo of bodies. He knew Ike couldn't make a run for it cuffed as he was, but he wasn't taking any chances with the killer. Everyone knew Ike was half crazy. He'd be even worse now, heading for a hanging.

Dickson pushed the horses double hard and fast. Time was not on his side and he knew it. After five days of brutal, non-stop riding, they exited the barren, twisted land of eroded buttes and treeless mesas, finally leaving the badlands behind. Ahead the first low hills began to rise. Beyond, blue in the distance, higher sawtoothed mountains swept the skyline. Up there someplace lay Fool's Gold, but Dickson began to question if Ike would ever make it that far, let alone Peralta. Each evening when they stopped for the day he had to physically haul Ike down out of the saddle. His legs were so weak he could barely walk. The smell of infection made it clear they were getting worse fast. At night the deadly game of staying awake started all over again with Dickson tying Ike's handcuffs under his legs, making it impossible for him to get to his feet even if he could. The long nights watching Ike while he slept made the next day's riding almost impossible. Dickson caught himself falling asleep several times in the saddle, only to wake with a start. Up front Ike twisted in the saddle, seeing the lawman struggling. He knew his chance to try and take him was coming soon. It had to be when they stopped for the night before they reached Fool's Gold. After that Peralta would be too close. So was the hangman Dickson promised would be waiting for him. Another five days of pushing horses higher through growing stands of dark pines left both men at the edge of endurance, bone-tired, desperate for rest. Even though Dickson had trained himself for years to need little sleep on long rides trailing other men, this was far different. He was wounded, in pain, unable to get any real sleep staying up all night watching Goss. Fighting off the maddening urge to give in to sleep became almost overwhelming. Ike was fighting deadly time too. He felt the soaring heat of a high temperature wracking his body in sweat as fever from infection grew worse. That evening when they stopped for the day to rest, he decided it was time to make his move while he still had enough strength left to do so.

Dickson hefted Ike off his horse, half dragging him to a clear spot under pines, still cuffed. He untied the pack horses, leading them to a stand of white-barked aspen a short distance away, leaving Emmett's and Virgil's bodies roped atop them. He wasn't sure he could heft them back up in the morning, he was so tired. Back with Ike, Dickson sat heavily taking in a deep breath, eyeing the brother. Another sleepless night of misery faced him while Ike got more rest and he had to watch. It was pure torture. Sleep, sweet sleep. If only he could get just one night of sleep he knew he'd make it to Fool's Gold. The little mining town had to be close by now.

'These irons are cuttin' into my wrists.' Ike's gravelly voice broke into his thoughts. 'At least put 'um up front so I can get me some sleep. My legs are gone. I can't run off no place crippled up like this. And make a fire, too. I don't want to freeze to death either. That's the least you can do if you want me to make it to Peralta.'

9

Ike sat back watching Dickson struggle gathering wood for a fire. It was obvious the star man was so tired he couldn't drag in more than a small pile. Once lit it crackled to life, Ike demanding relief again.

'You gonna change these cuffs up front or not? I'm bleedin' to death I tell ya!'

Dickson studied Ike for several seconds, debating with himself whether to take the chance or not. Leaning closer without answering, Dickson rolled Ike over on his back unlocking the steel bracelets. Pulling him back around they were face to face only inches apart. Ike's beady eyes bore into Dickson with daggers of pure hate. He saw how badly the lawman needed rest and sleep. Snapping the cuffs back on, Dickson had a warning.

'You so much as move, roll over or

try to get up and I'll kill you right where you sit. Understand me?'

'Yeah, I hear ya, law dog. You better get a good night's sleep, 'cause I will while you're havin' to sit up all night watching me.'

Ike laid down pretending to close his eyes while Dickson sat across flickering flames, shoulders stooped, watching him with his pistol in his lap. The meagre pile of firewood barely radiated enough heat to fight off the growing cold of the high country, but he was too tired to get up and search for more. Small flames gave off just enough light so that he could watch Ike. That's all that really mattered now. Dickson pulled his jacket collar higher, trying to get comfortable as time passed agonizingly slowly. The more he stared at Ike, the more his image became harder to focus on. Through dancing flames it looked like Ike was smiling back at him. When he cleared them it did not. His eyes ached so badly, all he wanted to do was get a few minutes' sleep. He rubbed his face, fighting to stay awake. The moment he stopped, the overpowering urge came right back again. He struggled another half hour as heavy eyelids began to close and his head dropped. This time he did not straighten up. Dickson gave in to deadly, dangerous, demanding sleep at last.

Ike peeked through slit eyes at the lawman. His chance had finally come. Ever so slowly, without making a sound, he pulled himself up on one elbow, as the fire burned lower. A club-size piece of wood stuck out of the flames. Gripping it, Ike carefully pulled it out, rolling on to his side, dragging himself inch by inch toward the sleeping man, never taking his eyes off him. Head down, chin on his chest, Dickson was deep in sleep and unaware Ike was closing in on him. Reaching Dickson's side, Ike dragged himself up on both knees, raising the burning club over his head with both hands, swinging it down with all his might on his head, sending the sleeping man crashing on to his back rolling on the ground, struggling to wake up from his worst nightmare. Ike struck again and again until Dickson rolled far enough away he couldn't reach him, staggering to his feet and searching wildly for the pistol laying next to the fire. Both men saw it at the same time. Both dove for it knowing the loser would die. Ike got his hands on it first, but Dickson dove on his back before he could use it, twisting it out of his hands, still riding him until he brought the six-gun down hard on Ike's head, knocking him unconscious.

The tall man slowly got to his feet, fighting for breath, bleeding and burned on his face. Hot coals smoked in his hair. He wildly brushed them out. Finding his feet and steadying himself he stared down at Ike, realizing how close he'd come to ending up dead. Kneeling, he unsnapped the handcuffs, rolling Ike over and locking them on his back again. That's a mistake he wouldn't make twice!

Ike awoke with blood running down his face from the gash on his head that felt like it would explode. There was another layer of pain before he realized he was laying hog-tied hands and feet, the rope tight around his neck nearly choking him.

'I . . . can't . . . breathe,' he gurgled, fighting for breath, as Dickson sat across the fire watching him.

'You better get used to it. That's the way you're going to stay until we reach Fools' Gold, or you die first!'

* * *

The fourth day after Ike's nearly successful attack, the two men rode out of timber to see a line of one-storey buildings up ahead situated in a small flat. Fool's Gold, at last. Blue smoke drifted up from a row of houses behind its single, dirt main street. On the sidewalk half a dozen men went about their business until the caravan of death reached the edge of town. They stopped, staring at the strange procession coming closer. Once on the main street, Dickson called out to the nearest men, 'You got a sheriff here?'

The trio walked into the street staring at him, then Ike, and the horses roped behind with their dead cargo. 'Sheriff? We ain't got no sheriff or even a jail if we did. Why's that man all hog-tied up like that? He's about blue in the face.'

'Don't you worry about him. I'm a US marshal, and he's in my custody. I need someplace where I can lock him up overnight while I get some sleep and maybe a little doctoring.'

'We ain't got no doctor either, 'cept maybe George Ames. He's no human doctor but a pretty good horse doctor. You say you're a lawman?'

'That's what I said. I need some help for a few hours with this man killer. He's Ike Goss, from Peralta, where he killed a freight wagon driver. I'm taking him back to hang for it.'

'Well, he looks like he's about half dead already. Could be he might not make it that far,' another bystander commented. 'Mind me asking what's those bodies roped on behind him?'

'That's his brothers, Virgil and Emmett. They were just as bad as he is. I've got another one to pick up before I reach Peralta.'

The growing knot of men looked at each other, digesting Dickson's cold remarks and attitude, until one spoke up. 'Bout the only thing we got that might hold a man is the meat house behind the blacksmith's shop. We keep ice in it to hang deer and elk meat. It's made pretty solid, and somebody tied up like that sure ain't goin' nowhere. That might work for you. Them other boys roped on those horses would have to stay outside though. We don't want that stink in there.'

'I don't think they'll mind. They're already on their way to hell,' Dickson answered.

'Come on then, we'll show you where it's at.'

After locking Ike in the meat house, Dickson tied off the brothers' horses around back with bodies still roped on them.

'Aren't you going to give them horses a rest and unload them?' one of the men asked.

'I'm too tired to do that right now. If any of you men are worried about it you can go ahead and take them off.' He looked from face to face. None volunteered to step forward. 'Like I said, I'll leave them on. I need to get some sleep. Keep this lock on until I wake up and don't anyone try to help Goss, no matter how hard or long he yells. He'll kill any of you if he gets half the chance. That's an official order.'

Dickson got directions to George Ames' small shack. As he stepped inside the house, Ames studied his burnt, scarred face, slowly shaking his head in amazement.

'You're a real mess. Anyone tell you I'm not a doctor?'

'Yeah, they did. But if you can do anything that helps that'll be at least something. I've still got the ride to Peralta ahead of me.'

'The boys tell me you're pulling a

caravan of dead men along with their live brother. Is that true or just whiskey talk?'

'It's true enough. And the live one is lucky he's not dead meat like the rest of them.'

'You must be a real hard man, Mr . . . ?'

'Ben Dickson. I'm a US marshal.'

'Well, Mr Ben Dickson, the way you treat life and death is just a little unusual even way up here in Fool's Gold. It doesn't bother you none to pull around dead men?'

'It does not and never has. That's my job, and I'm good at it. I've been doing it for a long time and plan to continue a while longer. Now do you have something to help my burns, or are we going to discuss my attitude about life, death and the law?'

Ames didn't answer, reaching for a jar on the shelf behind him and holding it up for Dickson to look at. 'I've got horse liniment and bear grease. Considering you're not a horse or any part of one, this bear grease is all I have. It might work until you get to a real doctor.'

'Let's try it. I need something to ease this pain.'

'We all have our own personal pain. That's why I like caring for horses. They don't complain nearly as much as most people do.'

Dickson studied the elderly man's lined face. He didn't answer this time. His inference was clear enough. Ames locked eyes with him as he started to apply the smelly grease. 'What do I owe you for this?' Dickson asked.

'You don't owe me a thing. I'm doing it out of human decency. You know anything about that, Mr Dickson?'

Without answering, the lawman left the Ames' house, making his way up the street to the cot house behind Somerset's Dry Goods store. Pushing inside he found an older woman sitting behind a small counter. She looked up, surprised to see a customer at this time of the day. Before she could utter a word, Dickson posed a question.

'Do you have someone working here or in your family that can stable my horse for me? I'll take the saddle-bags and shotgun off first. Right now what I need is sleep. I'll pay for whoever you have.'

She thought a moment. 'Ah, my son Jimmy can do it. What are you paying?'

'Two dollars is plenty. How soon can you get him over here?'

'He's in the house right behind here. It's another seventy-five cents for the cot and a blanket too.'

He pushed money over the counter. 'I don't want to be disturbed for any reason unless this place starts to burn down. You understand me?'

She nodded, handing him a small wooden disk with a number 5 on it. 'Your cot is way in back against the wall. You won't be bothered none there, no one else will probably come in until tonight anyway.'

He made his way into the shadowed room. The acrid smell of sweat from red dirt miners was thick in the air. At the cot he laid the saddle-bags down, using them for a lumpy pillow no one could touch without alerting him. Stretching out, boots still on, he pulled the shotgun up alongside and the blanket over him. He took in one long breath closing gritty, aching eyes. Before he could draw a second one Dickson was deep in exhausted sleep.

★　★　★

Maybe it was the thin stream of sunlight filtering through the walls, or the sound of shuffling feet close by that woke him up. Dickson pulled himself upright, still groggy. Kicking off the blanket he got to his feet, gathering the saddle-bags and shotgun, heading for the counter and finding it empty. Stepping outside into bright sunlight, he heard a door close behind him. Turning, he saw the counter woman exiting her house.

'How long have I been asleep?' he

asked as she came up.

She thought a moment, lifting her hand to her mouth, trying to count the hours. 'Ah . . . you came in yesterday morning and slept the rest of the day and last night too. I guess you slept that makes it . . . fifteen hours, maybe a little more?'

A sudden bolt of emotion shot through Dickson. It was the fear that Ike had enough time to somehow work himself free and escape. If anyone could, he was that man. Dickson started up the street at an uneven run. Reaching the meat locker, he drove the wooden peg locking the door bolt out, swinging the heavy door open. Ike lay on the floor still tied up, shivering uncontrollably, half conscious. Dickson breathed an audible sigh of relief, stepping inside.

'Wake up, Ike. We're riding all the way to Peralta. Let's get to it!'

Ike slowly opened his eyes. Instantly that glare of hate came back. His mouth quivered struggling for words, his face lined with excruciating pain. 'You . . . better . . . kill me. Right here . . . and now. Because, one way or the other . . . I will kill you.'

'Kill you? No, I'm going to enjoy watching the hangman do that. So is the rest of town while you dangle snapping and jerking.'

Ordering several men who came up to watch Ike, Dickson retrieved his horse from the stable. When he returned they helped boost Ike back on his horse while the tall man led the pair of horses behind the meat locker, carrying his brothers out front and tying them off to Ike's horse.

'I don't think your prisoner is going to make it all the way to Peralta, alive,' one man said, eyeing Ike slumped in the saddle.

'He'll make it all right. I'm going to see to it. I'm not going to let him die on me now. Not after what I had to do to run him down.'

The caravan of death rode down the street of Fool's Gold, disappearing into the timber at the trailhead at the end of town, while onlookers commented on their gruesome passage.

'That lawman Dickson treats his prisoner like he's an animal. I never heard of any marshal ever going that far, did you?' He looked to his friends.

'I'd say he's about as mean as they come. I sure wouldn't want him trailing after me, I know that for sure.' Another shook his head.

The star man pushed the horses hard again. Peralta lay only another two days ahead. He had to get there while Ike was still alive. His dream to ride down the main street pulling his dead brothers behind loomed even larger now that he was so close. The second morning on the trail Dickson reined off into a small flat studded with jack pines. Riding in a slow circle, his eyes covered the ground until finding a spot where cut limbs were scattered and bits of clothing, bone and one boot lay exposed. Easing out of the saddle, he moved them with his boot before looking up at Ike.

'You can say goodbye to your brother, Elwood. I left him here until I got back, but it looks like the wolves got to him first. There's nothing left to take.'

Ike's mouth twisted as he fought for breath and spittle ran down his wildly whiskered chin. 'You're . . . going to burn in hell.' He choked out the words. 'And it's . . . too damned good for the likes of you!'

'Maybe, but if I do you'll already be there to welcome me, won't you, Ike.'

Saddling up, Dickson pushed the caravan the rest of that day until near dark, when he was forced to stop. After hauling Ike down from his horse, he dragged in enough wood to make a fire that would last all night. As flames leapt to life, he sat opposite his prized prisoner, sizing him up one last time. Ike lay twisted on his side still hog-tied, still choking for breath.

'Get this damn rope . . . off my . . . neck. I can't . . . hardly breathe!'

Dickson considered the request without answering, debating with himself whether he should or not. After a lengthy pause he got to his feet, stepping around the crackling fire, rolling Ike over on his stomach, loosening the rope around his neck and using it to tie his feet together. The dying man coughed and swallowed, trying to catch his breath until he could speak again.

'Take 'em off my feet, too. Don't you know they're already dead? Have been for days. I can't feel nothin'. How dumb can you get!'

'It's staying on, dead or not. Tomorrow we'll reach Peralta, I want to be real sure you don't try anything before we do. Shut up and go to sleep. I want you all rested up when you meet your hangman.'

The lawman lay back on his saddle watching Ike intently. The long sleep in Fool's Gold had given him the strength and stamina he needed to make it through the night without nodding off.

The burning bullet wound in his chest would also keep him awake. When he was certain Ike had finally fallen asleep, he unbuttoned his jacket and shirt, pulling it open. The ugly wound was swollen and discoloured. Once they reached town he'd have to have the doctor treat it before it became any worse. Buttoning up he began thinking about all the days and weeks he'd travelled tracking down the Goss brothers from Peralta, over the mountains, all the way out into the badlands. He concluded this would be the longest chase he'd ever been on, even longer and more dangerous than tracking down renegade Apaches in Indian Territory, where he'd lost his leg. It was time to add it all up. Chambers and Mackenzie would have to pay the bill for it, the biggest pay day he had ever received.

While he sat congratulating himself, his thoughts turned to the old man, Vernal Goss. He wasn't finished with the Goss clan yet. When Vernal heard he was back in town with Ike towing his dead brothers behind him heading for a hanging, they would have it out one last time. Even twisted half-crippled Vernal was still as deadly as a den full of rattlers. He couldn't leave Peralta without riding out to the Goss ranch for one last showdown. The cold mountain night passed surprisingly fast as a blizzard of icy stars made their timeless arc across the black velvet sky, while Ben Dickson fed the fire, thinking about finally being able to head back home. He was certain when the tale of how he'd run down the Goss brothers got out it would spread like wildfire, enhancing his already legendary reputation as a fearless man tracker and killer. Once home he promised he'd take a long break and relax before taking on another job. He'd earned it after all this.

Dawn in the mountains always comes first and fast. Dickson sat jacket collar pulled high, feeding the fire the last stick of wood. A rosy glow in the eastern sky began silhouetting tall pines in stark black outline, as stars faded, finally blinking out to the brightening new day. He eyed Ike sleeping under a thin wool blanket. He was the prize, the last of the Goss brothers, the wildest and most dangerous of all. Today he'd parade him right down the middle of Main Street like a wild animal in a cage, for all to see. It would be the highlight of his long and successful career. He eased to his feet, stretching out the kinks with a low grunt of pain. Ben Dickson had seen a lot of dawns out on the trail after other men, but none like the one he was about to experience today. It was time to saddle up and cover the last miles to Peralta.

'Ike, wake up!' He kicked at his boots. 'Get up and let's get moving. Here comes tomorrow.'

10

Later that morning the timbered trail ran across an open saddle where Ike could look down the mountain seeing the image of the Goss ranch far below, still hidden in morning shadows. A tiny curl of blue smoke twisted up from the stone chimney. He knew Vernal and Hattie must be up. Ike strained to see it clearer. If he could only yell out for help. Somehow his father might hear him. The course rope cutting into his neck made that impossible. He tried twisting in the saddle as the scene faded away behind and his hopes sank with it. Dickson could see him squirming, knowing he could see the ranch, unable to do anything about it except suffer. That's exactly what he wanted Ike to do — and as much as possible in the few days he had left before his life would be choked out on a gallows.

The cool autumn sun cleared timber tops, lighting the trail starting steeply downhill. By late morning, Dickson could see the distant rooftops of buildings and houses beyond trees as they rode closer to Peralta. One final turn and they exited pines coming out on the dirt street at the far end of town. Dickson was about to make his promise to bring the Goss brothers back to justice a reality. Even before he reached the first buildings, people on the street began noticing the string of horses, pointing them out as others did too and the first knot of onlookers started up the street to meet the deathly caravan.

'Hey, that's Ike Goss!' someone shouted.

'Yeah, that's him all right. He looks all tied up like a Christmas turkey!' another commented, drawing tense laughter as men converged on the riders.

'Where'd you finally run him down, Marshal?' A voice came out of the milling throng of people.

'Is that all his brothers roped on in back?' A youngster ran up wide-eyed at all the excitement, staring up at Dickson.

Through all the shouted questions and comments, Dickson rode stoically forward without answering a single one. He'd waited a long time for this day and he wanted to end it in front of the mine men's office who hired him. Farther down the street more people spilled out of stores and businesses, building the crowd to larger proportions. When Dickson reined to a stop in front of the mining office, the street was filled boardwalk to boardwalk with excited, shouting men and a few women pointing and gesturing.

Rolo, sitting at his desk, heard the wild commotion outside. Getting to his feet he went to the window. One look at the wild scene and he shouted to his partner, 'Edward quick, let's get outside. Ben Dickson is back and you'll never believe who he has with him!'

Pushing through the door, Rolo's

face lit up in a broad smile. 'Ben, for God's sake we're glad to see you. I began to think something bad might have happened to you and maybe you weren't coming back, as much as I hate to admit it.'

Before Dickson could answer, Rolo's eyes fell on dirty, heavily bearded, bone thin Ike. He hardly recognized him.

'Here's the Goss brothers I promised you.' Dickson's voice broke his concentration, easing down. 'The two in back can't stand trial. They already tried killing me and lost. Elwood's dead too. The wolves took care of him so there was nothing to bring back. After you get someone to take care of these bodies and lock Ike up, I'll need a doctor. So will Goss, but only to keep him alive long enough until you can hang him.'

'Some of you men get Ike down and over to our wagon yard just outside of town,' Rolo ordered. 'We can lock him up in the powder house after I have my men clear it of caps and dynamite. How's that sound, Ben?'

'It'll do until you can build a gallows. And do it right here on Main Street so everyone can see him swing. He's earned a big crowd watching him go.'

'Shouldn't we at least have some kind of trial first?' Chambers interrupted. Several people in the crowd began echoing the same sentiment.

'Yeah, let's do it legal like,' a well-dressed man in a top hat shouted out. 'After all, Peralta is populated by decent, God-fearing citizens — aren't we? We're not a bunch of blood thirsty savages!'

Immediately conflicting opinions broke out as arguments for and against hanging Ike took sides. Shouting matches escalated into near fights as the mob began shoving and threatening each other before Rolo, on the boardwalk, raised his hands, shouting at the top of his lungs to stop the growing conflict.

'Listen to me, all of you. This man has just come back from nearly two months trailing the Goss brothers. I say we should let him decide how to handle this. After all, he faced them with guns blazing, didn't he? That gives him the right to have his say first. Be quiet and let's hear what Ben thinks.'

Dickson mounted the boardwalk tired, dirty and in pain. The bickering and infighting fired his short-fused temper. His eyes ran over the throng of men and women with disgust. What did these town people know or understand of cold, sleepless nights on the trail with little food, facing ambush and a bullet in the belly every minute, day and night? He took in a slow, painful breath, trying to contain his anger and not cuss the whole bunch of them out.

'Quiet!' someone shouted up front. 'All right, mister. What about it?'

'Every one of you here knows I'm a United States Deputy Marshal.' He paused long enough to let those words sink in. 'You also ought to know by now that I do what I say I'm going to do. I said I'd bring the Goss brothers back here to pay for what they did and here they are. There's no question that they killed John Standard, and robbed the freight wagon. I don't care which one of them pulled the trigger, they were all involved in it. Ike is the only one left alive, so he should pay for that murder. You don't have a court here in Peralta yet, and you don't even have a jail. If you have to wait for a line judge to show up that could takes weeks and even months. That could also mean lawyers get involved too. With those lily-fingered liars to defend him, Goss might only get a prison sentence instead of the hanging he deserves. You want to go through all that?'

The crowd erupted again in chaos; everyone began shouting and arguing until Dickson pulled his Colt, firing a single shot up into the air to stop them. As they quieted down, he continued. 'You want my opinion, here it is. I say hang Ike Goss, right here on Main Street next Sunday after church. It'll be a lesson no one will ever forget, and when the word gets around to other towns they'll know Peralta is no place to commit robbery and murder like these brothers did!'

This time no one could stop the raucous outbursts. Dickson let them go. He'd planted the seed he wanted, and it looked and sounded like it took root. He turned to Rolo and Chambers. 'I'm heading over to the doctor's office. I've got a chest wound that's giving me a lot of pain. Maybe he can do something for it. You two see to it Ike stays locked up until Sunday, and keep guards on him day and night. Then we'll conclude business about my fee and the time involved before I leave. Get these people going on a gallows too. The sooner they start the better.'

'Wait a minute, Ben.' Rolo put a hand on his shoulder. 'Even if they get it up and ready, we don't have anyone around here who wants to be a hangman. We've never done anything like that before.'

Dickson's cold stare bore into Mackenzie for several uncomfortable moments before he spoke. 'Don't worry about it. I'll hang him for you. And I won't even charge you extra for it.'

As the crowd thinned out, one old man in back still stood watching the tall man talking to Rolo and Chambers. White haired, half bent with age, Dell Berry was a long-time friend of the Goss family. He felt the same way about the sudden rise of the mine men buying up property all over the country running people off their land with the lure of money. Turning, he started up the alley to his mule, Jenny, tethered in back. He had urgent news for Vernal Goss. He meant to tell him about it as quick as Jenny could get him there. He knew Vernal wasn't going to let his son hang without trying to stop it, no matter who he had to kill to do it.

* * *

Hattie Goss was at the side of the house, feebly swinging an axe for firewood, when she saw Dell riding up the slope toward the ranch. She stopped, straightening up, glad to have some company and relief from Vernal's endless complaining. 'Dell,' she greeted with a tired smile, as Berry eased down off his mule. 'It's been a while since we've seen you. I'm sure glad you rode all the way out here. I know Vernal will be glad to see you too.'

'I don't bring good news. Hattie. I'd best tell it to Vernal first. Then he can tell you on his own. I'm sorry.'

Her tired eyes bore into him as her voice sunk to a whisper. 'Is it about my boys, Dell? If you know something please tell me. Don't be afraid. I've been waiting a long time wondering where they are and if they're all coming back home.'

Berry put both hands on her shoulders, looking down on the frail woman. 'All I'd say right now is it's about one of them. Don't ask me no more about it. It might be best you stay out here while I talk to Vernal. Where is he, Hattie?'

Vernal sat in the living room next to a sputtering fireplace, waiting for Hattie to bring in more wood. His usual blanket lay across useless legs trying to warm him. He heard footsteps coming

213

up the stairs outside. Twisting in the chair, he saw his old friend come through the door.

'Dell Berry! It's about time you came out to see an old cripple like me. Sit yourself down and let's talk a while.'

Berry walked across the room shaking hands before pulling up a chair and sitting face to face with Goss. He hesitated, trying to put the words right as both men stared at each other until Vernal finally spoke up.

'What is it? What's happened in town? I can tell by the look on your face it's some kind of trouble. Whatever it is, I need to know it.'

Berry straightened up, trying to avoid Vernal's searching stare. 'All right, here it is. That marshal named Dickson rode into town this morning. He had Ike with him hog tied on his horse, and the bodies of Virgil and Emmett, roped over their saddles. Dickson says he killed Elwood someplace up in the mountains. He's gonna hang Ike come Sunday morning after church right out on Main Street. I'm sorry to be the one who has to tell you all this, but I thought it best you hear it from a friend instead of strangers.'

Vernal's jaw dropped and his mouth trembled before uncontrollable shakes began wracking his entire body. He gripped the arms of the chair hard with both hands trying to stop it but couldn't. Dell leaned forward resting his hands over the old man's, trying to help until the tremors finally passed, and Vernal got his breath back. His lined face twisted red in rage, and his voice came out a sinister whisper.

'I . . . I . . . shoulda shotgunned him when I had the chance. It ain't too late yet, either. I'll kill him one way or the other, for what he's done to me and my family!'

Berry blinked hard, almost too scared to speak up. He took the risk anyway. He didn't want to see his old friend hurt any further — or worse, even killed himself.

'Vernal, we've been friends a long

time. I can't imagine the pain you're going through right now, but there's no way you can kill Dickson. I mean . . . you can't even get up out of that chair, much less into town. I know you want to avenge your boys, and I don't blame you one bit. There's no way that can happen. Don't torture yourself thinking about it. God takes care of men like Dickson. In due time, he will. You'll see.'

'I ain't waitin' for no fool God to do a damn thing. I said I'll kill him and I will. You better head on out of here, Dell. I've got to tell Hattie about her boys, and I don't want any company when I do.'

Berry got to his feet, looking down on his twisted old friend. He started to try to reason with him again, but stopped. Nothing he could say or do would help now. Dell was back outside on Jenny starting down the hill when he heard Hattie's anguished scream echoing down through timber. He didn't stop or look back.

That afternoon Doctor Orlay Mendelssohn adjusted his spectacles before carefully placing his slender white hands on Ben Dickson's chest wound, probing it slightly. When finished he looked up. 'Well, Mr Dickson, you're going to have considerable scar tissue because this couldn't be stitched up at the time of the wound, and it's too late now to try that. However, it seems to have healed up surprisingly well on its own. Did you use something on it? I see a slight residue of what looks like white powder?'

'I carry some medicine powders Indians gave me down in Arizona, a long time ago. They crush it from some kind of plants, using it on their own people. I've used it before, but not on something this bad. Out where I was I had no other choice. Have you taken a look at Ike Goss yet?'

'Yes, earlier this morning. He's dying, you know. Gangrene will take him quickly now. I'm actually surprised he's lasted this long. Most men would have died weeks ago.'

Dickson twisted on the examination table, peering through a curtained window barely able to see the gallows being built at the far end of town. 'They better hurry up with that scaffold. I want Ike to pay up in this world, not where he's going.'

Mendelssohn raised his eyebrows, taking a step back and studying his patient thoughtfully. 'You sound like a hard man, Mr Dickson. You have no pity for anyone?'

'They'll be none for me when my time comes. I don't waste sympathy on anyone else, either.'

The doctor shrugged, letting the subject drop. 'At any rate I think it's best you rest up and don't do anything strenuous. You don't want this wound to start bleeding again. That could cause trouble. I would also suggest you do no riding for at least another week or a bit longer. That could open the wound up again. I'd like to take a look at it in another three or four days.'

'I plan to be here at least until Sunday. After that I'll be gone. I've got some business to take care of tomorrow. Then I'm done in Peralta.'

Most Saturdays, the mine office was generally closed unless extra paperwork had to be dealt with. This Saturday was one of those exceptions, but not for paperwork. Rolo unlocked the door early that morning to allow Ben Dickson in. It was pay day for the extraordinary man-hunter and one he'd waited for a long time. He already had the figures in his head. He didn't need a pencil and paper to total them up.

'Morning, Ben.' Chambers came across the room and shook hands. 'How's that chest wound coming along? Better, I hope.'

'The doctor says another week and I'll be good as new, but I won't be here. You two ready to lighten that cash in your safe?'

'We are,' Rolo answered, also shaking hands. 'What exactly do we owe you for all you've done? Edward and I have a figure, but we want yours to see if we're correct.'

'I'm sure you remember the original fee we agreed upon was four hundred dollars per man whether I bring them in dead or alive?'

'We do,' Mackenzie nodded.

'You'll have to take my word for it that I took care of Elwood. The wolves got to his body before I could bring him back. That makes three, him, Virgil and Emmett dead. Ike will be tomorrow when I hang him. I'm doing that one for free, something I rarely do. I get paid for men I take down, but Ike is a special case. I personally want to see him die for all the trouble I had to go through tracking them all the way into the badlands for nearly two months plus this wound. I'll count that as a personal pleasure. Four hundred times four comes to sixteen hundred dollars. Is there any disagreement with that number from either one of you?'

'None whatsoever,' Rolo agreed. 'We've got your money right here in the safe. Do you want bills or silver and gold?'

'I only take coin. I don't trust paper. It burns, tears and flies away in the wind. I like the heft and jingle of real cash.'

'Good enough.' Edward went to the safe, twisting the dial until the heavy steel door swung open. Reaching inside he withdrew two steel trays lined with glittering coins and three large leather pouches. Back at the counter, he carefully counted out the money. 'Do you want to count it before I sack it up, Ben?'

'I'm counting with you. I can see what's going in.'

As Chambers tied off the top of each pouch, he looked up at Dickson. He had a question that had been haunting him since the lawman first rode back into town with Ike towing his dead brothers. 'Do you mind if I ask you something?'

'Likely not, you're paying for it.'

'Would you tell us exactly how you

managed to finish off all three brothers and still stay alive yourself? It's hard for us to even imagine something like that.'

'There really isn't much to tell. Men on the run are always at a disadvantage. They're always looking back wondering if someone like me is gaining on them or going to show up in the middle of the night. They lose sleep at night making poor decisions that grow worse every day. The Goss brothers were no different. Because Ike was the leader and meanest of the three, he's the one I think killed John Standard. He lasted the longest because he's like his father, Vernal, but not long enough to outsmart me. He's getting no older than tomorrow. I'm going back to Birdie's now to begin packing up. It's been profitable doing business with you two even if it did take longer than I originally thought. I'll see you tomorrow at the rope party.'

The tall man exited the office, closing the door behind him as Rolo and Edward stood looking at each other until Mackenzie went to the window watching Dickson secure the pouches in his saddle-bags before saddling up and riding down the street, out of sight. He turned back to his partner, shaking his head in amazement.

'It's still hard for me to imagine a man like that with a soul cold as ice. When it comes to life and death, it's all nothing more than a business deal. He even looks forward to hanging Ike. I've never heard of anyone like that. In a way, I hope I never do again. It's scary. There is just something about his attitude that frightens me even though we've called him friend for this short time. I know I'd hate to call him our enemy, that's for sure. He thinks nothing of taking anyone's life for the right price.'

Edward cast a long, silent stare at his partner before responding. 'You do remember it was you and me that hired him, don't you? We wanted a man to find John's killer, and agreed to pay for it. Does that make us any better than he is? I don't think so. Some might call what we did paying Dickson blood money. Our hands aren't clean in all this because we didn't pull the trigger. We're as much part of it as he is. That's the way I see it. Now that it's over I guess I'm having some second thoughts myself. I'll be glad when tomorrow is over. I can't say I'm looking forward to watching Ike hang or anyone else either. I want it over and done with. Maybe then we and this town can get back to normal. Whatever that is.'

Rolo nodded, slowly letting his partner's words sink in. 'So will I, Edward. This whole thing has gotten a lot more brutal than I ever thought we'd be part of.'

11

Vernal Goss spent all Saturday night sitting up in the living room, wrapped in his blanket trying to somehow devise a plan that might save Ike. As the first thin streaks of Sunday morning brightened the sky over the mountains behind the house, he'd made up his mind on one dangerous, daring idea. The more he went over it, the more he became convinced it could work, but he'd need help. Dell Berry had given him the schedule for Ike's hanging. Timing, Vernal knew, had to be the key. Ben Dickson might think he was going to hang the last of his boys tomorrow, but if Vernal had his way it meant Dickson would never see Monday dawn alive.

'Hattie,' he called out to his wife, still in the back bedroom. 'Get up and in here. I'll need your help.'

The little woman rolled over fighting

to wake up, her husband's insistent voice echoing throughout the empty house. Pulling herself up she tried rubbing sleep out of her eyes, wondering what he wanted at this early hour. 'I'm coming, Vernal. Just give me a minute to get something on.'

'Hurry up. We can't waste no time. We've got lots to do!'

Coming into the living room still fighting off heavy eyes, she ran hands through her thinning white hair. 'What is it, what's the matter, Vernal? Did you have another bad night with the shakes again?'

'No. I want you to help me get my pants and boots on, then hook up the buckboard. Can you do that by yourself? Remember how I showed you?'

The sudden blizzard of questions stunned Hattie. She tried to make some sense of it all. Coming up to the chair she put a hand on his shoulder, trying to calm him.

'Why would you want me to do that, Vernal? You're not going anyplace and neither am I. I'll fix you something warm to drink. Maybe you'll feel better.'

'I don't want somethin' to drink! Listen to me. Help me get dressed and get the buckboard ready. I'm goin' to town and you're gonna stay right here when I do.'

'Going to town? What on earth for? You haven't been in Peralta in six months, and said you'd never go back last time.'

'Stop tellin' me what I said and just do what I want. I'm goin' in to get Ike, before Dickson hangs him!'

Hattie let out a small cry of fear, both hands suddenly raised to her mouth as tears began running down her ashen face. She tried to say no, but the sudden lump in her throat choked off the words.

★   ★   ★

Ben Dickson woke that morning to a knock on his bedroom door at the boarding house. 'It's 6:45, Mr Dickson,' the house boy's muffled voice announced. 'Miss Birdie will have breakfast on the table pretty quick, sir.'

Dickson sat up, starting to stretch and catching himself from a sudden burst of pain burning across his chest. Once up he began to dress, satisfying himself today would end his stay in Peralta, and finish off the last of the Goss brothers too. He thought back over the long weeks he'd been forced to spend trailing and killing Elwood, Virgil and Emmett, to make this day a reality. Watching the fear in Ike's eyes when he tightened the rope around his neck would make up for all of it. Finished dressing, he went to the enamelled basin atop the cabinet washing his hands and face, starting to comb long, black hair. The reflection in the mirror made him pause, studying himself close up. Deep lines born of age, long trailing and vicious gunfights, radiated out around his eyes and mouth. The first few silver strands showed at his temples and sideburns. He straightened up, stopping his self inspection. It was time to go downstairs and eat breakfast, not start questioning the steady advance of years and his own mortality. He had a hanging to take care of.

Birdie was already seated with several new faces around the table. She stared at the lawman thoughtfully while passing a platter of bacon and eggs over. 'I guess you know the whole town is talking about the hanging this morning. They say you're also the one who is going to do it. Is that so, Mr Dickson, or only saloon talk?'

'I am.' He began eating, looking back at her, waiting for more questions he could see in her eyes.

'I don't want to pry, but do you find it difficult to enjoy a meal when you know you're going to actually hang someone?'

'I do not. I'm doing a civic duty. Yours and everyone else here in Peralta, who doesn't have the backbone to carry it out themselves. Who better than a man of the badge like me? I took a bullet for it. Pass the toast and coffee if you don't mind, and let's have less conversation.'

He calmly continued eating while all

eyes around the table fell on him. A middle-aged woman at the far end grabbed her child by the hand, getting up. 'I won't let my daughter hear talk like this. What kind of a town is this that can feed a hangman? We'll eat breakfast after this man is gone. I'm surprised you'd even seat him with decent people!' She exited the room glaring at Birdie.

'Before I leave I'll pay you what I owe. This will be my last day in town,' he informed Birdie, who only nodded saying nothing, continuing to watch him out of the corner of her eye.

Chambers and Mackenzie shared a large cabin just outside town. Neither man was married. The arrangement worked perfectly well for both men. On orders from Dickson, they'd had three of their most trusted workers watch over Ike Goss day and night. They fed him twice a day, checked to see his handcuffs were still tight, and helped stand him up when he had to answer the call of nature. Rolo started warming up the fire in a big potbellied stove, putting on a fresh pot of coffee to boil.

'You want breakfast?' he asked.

'Not me, not today.' Edward shook his head, sitting up on the bed and pulling on socks and boots. 'I just want Monday to come and all this be over.'

'Me too. I guess when we hired Ben Dickson, I never thought it would all end like this and we'd have to be part of a hanging.'

'No one could have. When all this is over and done with we have to lead the effort to get a full-time sheriff here in town. We can't do this again.'

* * *

Ike opened his eyes at the sound of the steel door creaking open in the powder house. Two men pushed in with a tray of food, while a third stood outside, shotgun in the crook of his arm.

'Here's your last breakfast. We'll stay right here until you finish it.'

Ike rolled over struggling to sit up,

glaring at the pair. 'I can't eat nothin' with these cuffs on. You'll have to take at least one off.'

'We can't do that. Orders are you're to stay cuffed up both hands.'

'Orders, what orders? Did that two-bit law dog Ben Dickson tell you that? If he told you to go out and shoot your horses, would you two fools do that too?'

'Listen Goss, John Standard was a good friend of mine and a lot of other people here around town. You murdered him in cold blood, when you and your brothers could have just robbed the freight wagon and let him be. Instead you shot him down like a sick dog. You can either eat this breakfast or starve. I don't care which it is. I've got no sympathy for you either way.'

Ike grabbed the tray, and tossing it across the room, cussing out the pair as they stepped back outside, slamming the door shut behind them leaving him in the dark to his muffled shouts of defiance.

★ ★ ★

Vernal checked the clock on the fireplace mantel, as Hattie finished pulling on his boots, talking in low whispers of desperation to herself.

'It's already 8:30. You gotta help me out to the buckboard. You got it ready?'

'I think I got it hooked up right, but won't you please stop and listen to me, Vernal? You can't do this. This crazy idea of yours will only get you killed, too. Our boys are already gone. I can't make it without you by myself. Can't you see that?'

He reached down, pulling her up until their faces were only inches apart. 'No, Hattie, you listen to me. I've got no life left in me. I haven't had one since my legs got crushed under that wagon years ago. All I can do is sit here every day, all day, wonderin' why it happened. At least now I've got one reason left to do somethin' any man would do to save his own flesh'n' blood.

Git me up and out into the buckboard. Bring out my bag of shotgun shells too.'

Hattie nearly buckled under his weight and lack of balance as both hung on to each other until he stopped shaking, putting the shotgun under his arm for a crutch, steadying himself enough to take one small step after another out the front door. He had to rest before trying the stairs, step by excruciating step until reaching the bottom, where he nearly crumpled as she fought to keep him up. He rested again before reaching the buckboard, grabbing the seat rails, pulling himself up inch by inch into the seat while she shoved from behind. Once seated Vernal grabbed the reins, breathing heavily, looking down on her.

'Git me that bag of shotgun shells. I've got to go. If I don't came back, you hav'ta know you're the only thing that kept me going all these years. Understand?'

She looked up and for that brief moment, the love they once shared as a young couple returned. She gripped his arm tight as he asked again to retrieve the canvas pouch. Handing it up to him, tears streaked her pleading eyes.

'Please, Vernal, don't do this. It can't work. Stay here and help me bury our boys like we should. I don't want to have to do that to you, too.'

'The only one going to git buried is Ben Dickson. And I'm gonna do it before he can kill Ike. Step back, Hattie!'

The buckboard rattled away as Vernal cracked the whip, while she stood watching it disappear down through tall pines. Her head dropped. She began to sob again walking back to the stairs, collapsing with her head in both hands, fearing an end she could not stop.

★ ★ ★

One block back of Main Street and the newly finished gallows, pastor Nils Sonderman slipped into his clothes, preparing to lead his thin flock of

235

parishioners in the First Lutheran Church's Sunday service. But this would be unlike any other Sunday Service he'd ever given. The good pastor was up against a real problem, uncertain exactly how to frame his godly sermon at the same time a brutal public hanging was going to take place.

He went to a mirror, beginning to carefully trim his bright red beard. The face he saw staring back was blank with an answer to his dilemma. His problems were further compounded by the fact he was unsure how many of his meagre flock would actually attend, choosing instead to watch the hanging. Finishing the scissor work he turned away, going to a small desk in one corner of the room, sitting retrieving paper and pen trying to find inspiration for his sermon. A glance at the clock on a shelf next to him showed he had little time left to come up with something relevant. It was already 9:15.

★　★　★

Dickson packed up his personal belongings, paying off Birdie Lee, before leaving without so much as a goodbye. Pulling the door shut behind him, she went to the front room window to watch the tall man walk away with saddlebags over his shoulders, and a shotgun in one hand. What a cold emotionless man, she thought, hoping never to meet anyone like him again. She was just as certain she would not attend the hanging that was on everyone's lips. Let the gawkers and morbidly curious do that. No decent woman in Peralta would. Birdie Lee was certainly that.

At the livery stable Dickson settled his account, saddling his horse, tying saddle-bags on before shoving the scattergun into its scabbard. Once in the saddle he rode slowly up the street to the newly built gallows, where a crowd was already beginning to gather. Dismounting, he climbed the steps while everyone watched in quiet fascination. 'You ready to swing, Goss?' one bold voice shouted out.

'Yeah, bring him on and let's get to it,' another demanded.

Up the street, walking toward the knot of people, Edward glanced at his partner. 'You ready for this?'

'I guess I am. I know I never want to attend another hanging once this is over.'

Reaching the circle of onlookers, both men edged through people until they were up front next to the wooden scaffolding looking up at Dickson. A man standing next to Rolo nudged him in the ribs with a question.

'You going to spring that trap? You may as well. You two paid to run Goss down.'

A small ripple of laughter came from those close enough to hear, as Rolo vigorously shook his head no. Dickson heard it too, looking down on the mine men.

'You want to come up here with me?' he asked.

Both said they did not. Dickson turned away, stepping on the trap door to test it with his weight. It didn't budge. Backing off, he grabbed a thick wooden handle protruding up from the floor. With one firm yank he pulled it back and the trap door snapped open with a sharp clang, exposing the free fall to eternity twelve feet below. A shout of approval rang out from the crowd. Dickson pulled his pocket watch to check the time: 9:18.

'It's time for you two to get Ike.' He looked down again on Rolo and Edward. 'If you want a bible thumper to say his last words, you better do that too. I don't want Ike to be late for his appointment in hell.'

Rolo turned to his partner. The look of defeat already on his face made it clear he wanted no part of bringing Ike back.

'Edward, I'll go see Pastor Sonderman, if you'll have our men bring Ike in. I don't want to see him up close if I don't have to.'

Chambers understood, putting a hand on Rolo's shoulder. 'All right. I'll

239

get him. You see Sonderman.'

The pastor was still hunched over his desk trying to produce a sermon that could balance out the brutality of a public hanging with the word of God. He'd only written three disjointed lines when a knock on the door of his small house in back of the church broke what little concentration he had. Getting to his feet, he crossed the room and opened the door.

'Hello, Pastor.' Mackenzie forced a thin smile, hoping he could convince Sonderman to agree with his unusual request at short notice. 'My name is Rolo Mackenzie. My partner and I own the mining company here in town. Our office is on Main Street, not far from your church here.'

'Sunday service is at ten o'clock, Mr Mackenzie. I'm very busy right now. If you'd care to attend then, we'd appreciate you joining us.'

'Yes, I know that. I'm not here for the service. There's a request for you to attend the hanging of Ike Goss this morning to give him his last words of comfort. You being the only church in town, they've asked me to see if you'd officiate, sir. They're bringing him over to the gallows right now. If you could come with me I'm sure everyone would be most grateful for your presence and words of comfort.'

Sonderman stared back, overwhelmed as he considered this strange and sudden turn of events. It instantly dawned on him that this was his one way out of the dilemma that haunted him since he sat down at the desk trying to come up with a meaningful sermon. The Lord had come to his rescue. It would be the perfect way to salvage his Sunday service! Sonderman's eyes lit up. He seemed to suddenly grow a little taller at the redemption of it all.

'Why yes, I'll attend and give this poor soul some final words of comfort. First, I'll have to take a moment to write a note for the front door of my church, so everyone knows where I'll be. The faithful will want to come too, brutal as all this may seem. It will be a wonderful abject for those who might consider straying from the word of God.'

'Please hurry. We don't have much time. It's nearly ten now.'

Chambers rode up to the powder house and saw the guards standing by the front door, watching him. 'It's time to get Ike out,' he ordered, getting down. 'Unlock it and let's get to it.'

'I don't think he can walk that far,' the man with the shotgun volunteered. 'His legs are about gone. We might have to prop him up or carry him.'

'Do what you have to, even if we have to put him on my horse.'

The heavy steel door squeaked open to reveal Ike sitting up on the floor, hands still cuffed, filthy dirty, hair wildly sticking out. His body was down to skin and bones. The sudden burst of light caused him to turn away squinting, as the guards stepped in pulling him to his feet where he quickly collapsed. Chambers' face grew grim at the sight of him. He barely looked like a man that had murdered John Standard.

'Put him on my horse. I'll lead it on foot,' Edward motioned.

Ike stared back through sunken eyes filled with hate. 'You people . . . think you're better than me or my kin. You call us trash . . . you're the real animals, and now you know it. Go ahead and prove it!'

Chambers didn't answer. He couldn't. There was too much truth in what Ike said. He silently wished Dickson had killed Ike somewhere out in the wilderness instead of bringing him back here to town, forcing Rolo and him to witness his hanging. He never imagined things would end like this.

The guards kept Ike in the saddle, riding close alongside him keeping him from falling off, while Chambers led the horse into town. The crowd began talking excitedly as they came into view, the same moment Pastor Sonderman mounted the gallows steps alongside Dickson.

'Are you the man to take Mr Goss

into the hereafter?' he whispered under his breath.

'I'm judge, jury and executioner,' the tall man announced without looking at Sonderman, whose eyes were locked on Ike as the horseman rode up to the gallows. 'Get him up here!' Dickson ordered in a loud voice. The crowd suddenly quietened to witness Ike's final moments. The guards lifted him off his horse, carrying him up the steps, forced to hold him upright to stop him from sinking to his knees.

'Hold him steady while I put this rope around his neck.' Dickson pulled the noose down over Ike's head adjusting the knot at the back of his neck, their faces inches apart.

'Now let's see what you're made of, Ike!' Dickson hissed.

Ike twisted his head around spitting a gob of stinking goo across Dickson's face.

'That's how tough . . . you bastard!'

Dickson stepped back, wiping his face with the back of his shirt sleeve, eyes still locked on Ike's. 'All right, Pastor, have your little say and make it fast.'

Sonderman stepped forward putting a hand on Ike's shoulder, secretly thrilled to be in front of the largest audience he'd ever had. 'Dearly beloved, we ask our Lord God to forgive this man, Ike Goss, his earthly sins . . . '

Down at the end of the street there was the sudden sound of a commotion as a buckboard careered wildly toward the crowd, totally out of control with Vernal Goss whipping the horse with one hand, holding a shotgun in the other.

'Look out!' someone shouted.

'He ain't stopping!' another screamed, people scattering for the boardwalks at a run, trying to keep from being run over.

12

'Kill 'em Paw, kill 'em all!' Ike shouted, the buckboard racing dangerously closer, Vernal lifting the shotgun to fire. Dickson dived for the floorboards but not Sonderman, who still stood bewildered by the sudden violence. Buckshot cut into his face and neck, killing him instantly; he fell backwards, Bible flying from his hands, his body collapsing on the trap door lever, springing it open. Ike dropped straight down. The soggy snap of his neck was lost to the thunder of Vernal's second shot that racked the platform. Dickson rolled to his knees pulling his big Colt, firing three fast shots and hitting the old man twice. The reeling buckboard crashed into the gallows, bouncing off as the terrified horse continued running wildly down the street with its dead driver sprawled backwards over the seat.

Excited people rushed back into the

street up to the gallows, pointing and yelling at the disappearing buggy. Rolo and Edward forced their way to the front of the throng, looking up at Dickson.

'Ben — are you all right, are you hit?'

The tall man back on his feet holstered the Colt, shaking his head, turning to the pastor, surveying his bloodied body and the tight rope swinging slowly back and forth down the trap door hole. Looking down at the mine men, he made only one brief remark.

'The Good Book didn't do him much good, did it? I took care of Ike like I said I would. You get the old man for free. That seals our deal!'

* * *

The following morning the sound of hammers and double jacks resounded up and down the quiet streets of Peralta. The gallows were coming down as three carpenters began dismantling

247

them beam by beam, board by board. One of the men atop the highest beam untied the hanging rope. Coiling it up in neat loops, he glanced at his pals below.

'Hey, one of you want this hangman's rope?'

The three looked up at this eerie question.

'No, we don't want it. Maybe them mine men up the street would. They paid for it didn't they?'

'That's so,' the top man answered. 'When we're done here I'll take it to them.'

Vernal's buckboard was retrieved two miles outside of town later that same morning. He and Ike were buried the next day side by side, in the town's small cemetery in a shaded clearing surrounded by tall pines. Only Dell Berry, Hattie and two grave diggers attended. Dell tried to say a few words of comfort as the coffins were being lowered, but Hattie's quiet sobbing stopped him.

'Come on, Hattie.' He led her by the arm toward his buggy. 'I guess there's no more to really say. They're gone and nothing's going to change it. I'll take you back home.'

The shovel men leaned on their tools, waiting respectfully for the buggy to go out of sight. As it disappeared down through trees, the only sound that could be heard was the soggy thud of fresh earth hitting the top of two pine coffins as the men bent their backs to their final task.

Reaching town, Hattie put her hand on Dell's arm, requesting him to stop at Mackenzie and Chamber's office on Main Street.

'Why on earth would you want to do that?' His face was an open question.

'Just do it, Dell. I'll explain it later.'

At the office Berry pulled to a stop, getting down to help Hattie up on to the boardwalk. 'You sure you don't want me to come in with you?'

'No.' She shook her head. 'This won't take long. Just wait a few minutes for

249

me. I've got to do this alone.'

'Well, all right. If that's the way you want it.' He stepped back in confusion, watching her reach the front door.

Edward Chambers was working at his desk when Hattie stepped inside. Rolo was out back gathering fresh firewood for the pot-bellied stove. Chambers quickly came to his feet approaching the counter, expecting to be assaulted by the wrath of the tiny woman. Instead she took in a slow breath, levelling a gaze on him for several uncomfortable moments before speaking.

'I won't bandy words with you,' she began. 'More than once you made the offer to my husband to buy our place out in Goss Canyon. You still want it?'

Edward stood flabbergasted, turning red in the face, trying to clear his throat to answer. 'I'm . . . sorry about your husband, Mrs Goss. Rolo and I never meant for anything like that to happen.'

She waved off his apology. 'I didn't come to hear that. Do you want to buy or not?'

'Can I ask after all that's happened why you're offering it to us now?'

'I'm leaving Peralta, for good. I've buried my sons and husband. There's nothing left here for me. I'll use the money to get back home to Missouri, and what's left of my family there. You come out tomorrow morning and I'll sign off the deed, but only for the same amount of cash money you offered Vernal.'

Rolo stepped through the back door with an armload of firewood. Seeing Hattie, he stopped in his tracks glancing at Edward. Before he could ask the obvious question his partner spoke.

'Mrs Goss wants to sell us her ranch in Goss Canyon. I told her we'd be glad to buy it from her.'

Mackenzie couldn't answer. It was too much to try and understand so quickly. He dumped the wood next to the stove, coming to the counter, never taking his eyes off the tiny white-haired woman.

'Are you sure you want to do that?'

He parroted Edward's question.

'We raised up four boys out there and for a while we were a happy family. After my husband got crippled in that freight accident, everything changed. He changed. He became bitter and mean about everything, including us. When you two came around offering to buy our place I asked him to sell so we could take the money and try to make a new start someplace else, but he wouldn't hear of it. It only made him worse. I'm all that's left now. I want to be as far away from here as I can get. If Vernal had listened to me in the first place none of this killing would have ever happened. You two be out to my place in the morning and bring cash. I don't want no cheque.'

Hattie turned, walking out the door, leaving Rolo and Edward staring after her then at each other, speechless at the amazing turn of events.

★ ★ ★

Ben Dickson left Peralta unnoticed and unseen early the following morning after Ike's hanging. His saddle-bags were heavy with gold and silver coins. He'd finally finished the contract he originally thought would take only a few weeks that instead lasted months. He looked forward to returning to Arizona, and his permanent room at the Double Hot Hotel. He needed a rest and knew it. It had been a long and difficult task trailing the Goss brothers and his still-painful chest wound had taken its toll on his energy and endurance, as much as he hated to admit it to himself. Now he looked forward to long quiet afternoons sitting on the hotel's front porch in his favourite chair, sipping an occasional tequila.

Rincon Valley was a long ride south. He meant to enjoy the leisurely pace getting there. No more schedules to meet and no deadly men to face with flaming six-guns. As each day passed he even surprised himself how much he enjoyed the natural pace of it. He also vowed that once he reached home he would not take another job for a while. Exactly how long, he wasn't sure yet. He'd make that call when he felt fit and ready. A week into his ride it dawned on him he had a birthday coming up soon in October, his forty-second. It seemed life could not get much better.

* * *

Tales of the unbelievable exploits of Ben Dickson, especially his time in Peralta, travelled far and wide from small mountain towns across the west, down to flat land farms and even cities back east. Popular dime novelists that had never seen him and never would, began writing about Dickson in glowing terms as a man tracker and killer without peer. The public's appetite for the wild stories grew enormous. One of those writers was Lewis Lansing, who sat in the offices of the *Gentleman's Gazette* on Madison Street in Chicago.

Lansing had a large and popular following in the *Gazette*. Now he had a red-hot idea how to make that even larger. Behind the big oak desk across from him sat Horace Throckmorton, owner and publisher of the *Gazette*, his thin white hands folded across a ponderous stomach, as Lansing enthusiastically pitched his exciting new idea.

'Listen boss, we can make a fortune running Sunday supplements about this man Ben Dickson, then follow it up with a book about his life as a paid-for hired killer. If you'll open up your wallet and put up the money for me to go out west I'll find him and get that story. It cannot miss. It's a natural best seller. You can use the Sunday stories as the teaser, then bring the book out after a few months.'

Throckmorton leaned back in his big padded chair without comment, thinking the whole idea over. He knew Lansing was a well-known and well-liked writer in the *Gazette*. The book idea did intrigue him, but there were clearly risks, financial ones, and if there was anything he kept under tight control it was the nickels and dimes that could suddenly add up to thousands of dollars going in the wrong direction if you weren't always cautious and careful. He probed a bit further.

'Exactly where out west does this famous gun fanner live?' He leaned forward for an answer, pursing his lips.

'I'm told he lives in Arizona. Someplace called Rincon. I can't find it on any of our maps, but there must be a town or city someplace close to it. This is the chance of a lifetime. We can scoop all the other publishers. He just tracked down and killed an entire family of murderers. I think their name was Goss, or something that sounded like that. They were four sons and their old man. He killed them all! Now is exactly the time for us to capitalize on the stories going around about him. What do you say, boss? Let me give it a try.'

Careful, penny-pinching Mr Throckmorton rested his double chins on one hand, calculating the time and expense to send Lansing all the way down to Arizona. His eyes settled on a picture hanging on a wall behind Lansing. The large, lavishly-coloured oil painting depicted a cowboy riding full out at night in a rain storm. A sudden bolt of lightning streaked down the background, while he chased a herd of stampeding cattle. Horace had always loved that picture. It was an adventure he always wished he could live, if someone could get him up on a horse big enough to carry him. He looked back at his writer, weighing the chancy odds of success.

'Tell you what, Lansing. I'll give you one month to find this man and sign him to a book deal. You tell him I'll offer a twenty-five per cent royalty on every book sold, but I won't pay any advance money, especially since we're spending all the money taking the risk of me sending you there. We don't even know if he can sign his own name, let alone coherently recite his life story. You and I both know how most of those western gun slingers really turn out to be. They are back-shooting brutes who kill from ambush that should have been hung rather than praised. Be that as it may, if this story is as good as you think it is, we may have something here worth publishing. I trust for your sake it is. I'd hate to have to fire you for spending all this time and my money on a wild goose chase. Do I make myself clear?'

'You sure do, and don't worry. You won't be sorry. I'm going to bring back a story that will knock your socks off. We'll get rich over it . . . or at least you will, boss.'

*   *   *

After Mackenzie and Chambers paid off Hattie Goss, she immediately left town as she'd vowed. The two men took a half dozen of their workers out to the old house in Goss Canyon, with orders to burn it to the ground so exploratory work could begin on mining the site. In the glow of the fiercely burning fire, both men stood thinking of all the misery and death that led to this moment, wondering if it had really been worth it. At last they had the property, but at what cost in human life? As the last wall came crashing down in a cloud of sparkling embers, neither man could be sure hiring Ben Dickson had been the right thing to do after all.

Three weeks later, work at the new exploratory mine shaft revealed the richest vein of nearly pure silver Rolo or Edward had ever seen. The desperate, destitute Goss family had been sitting on top of a fortune that would run into the millions of dollars, never knowing it. As more land was cleared on the property, workers also discovered the hidden money from the robbery and murder of John Standard. That find made both men conclude everything had finally come full circle, easing the guilty conscience they'd both been struggling with over all the killings.

★ ★ ★

Lewis Lansing sat at the window of the Canton & Keller stagecoach, peering out at the jagged peak of Mica Mountain, dominating the skyline. The driver had already informed him once they topped out at Ridington pass, they'd start the downhill run into Rincon Valley. Somewhere only a few miles away should be the tiny, isolated village of Double Hot. Coach wheels slowed as the whip man eased back on the reins, applying brakes to steel shod wheels, reaching the summit. Lansing pulled out a handkerchief, mopping sweat from his face again in the blistering heat. He couldn't imagine how or why anyone would live in a land that always seemed to breathe fire, compared to his home far to the north in cold, windy, snowbound Chicago.

Lansing was a man running out of time and he knew it. It had taken him far longer than originally planned or promised to get this far. He had to find

260

Ben Dickson as fast as possible. Much to his disappointment he'd only recently learned there really was no town named Rincon, Arizona, only the Rincon Mountains surrounding the valley of the same name, making finding Dickson even more difficult. By the afternoon it was well on its way to being another one hundred degree day, when the stage rocked to a stop at the valley floor. Lansing leaned out the window at the shout of the driver.

'This is it. You're in Rincon Valley. There's a small cattle ranch about half mile down that road.' He pointed. 'You can likely rent a horse there to ride to Double Hot.'

'Doesn't this stage go there?' His voice was strained with disappointment.

'Nope. No reason to. There's nothing there but a few adobe buildings, and an old hotel. We couldn't make a plug nickel. You're on your own from here. Good luck!'

★   ★   ★

261

Ben Dickson was relaxing on the shaded front porch of the hotel, when he saw the lone figure of a rider atop a mule coming out of brush and thorny cactus still some distance away. He eyed the rider curiously until he pulled to a stop at the hitching rail, recognizing him as a teenage kid named Zac Wild. Wild was part of a big family that lived several miles away in the brushy mesquite flats struggling to eke out a living with a few bony longhorn cattle and half wild horses. Already nearly six feet tall with an odd hunched-over walk, Zac looked like an old man at a distance. Dickson had seen him before, never paying much attention to the illiterate kid. The only thing that made him look different this time was a pistol stuffed in his pants top, hanging out at an odd angle.

'Howdy ... Mr Dickson.' Zac stepped up on the porch, looking down at Dickson with his usual half smile on his pimply face.

'Hello, Zac. What are you doing here in town?'

'Well . . . I'm eighteen now and Paw says I can ride in here and have me a drink of that mescal, if I want . . . because I'm a man now.'

'I see you're carrying a pistol for the first time.'

'Yup. Paw gave it to me. He says I'm grow'ed up enough to have one.'

'A man, huh? There's a lot more to being a man than carrying a six-gun. You also have to be man enough to back it up if it comes to that. It might be best you leave that old iron at home a while longer, before walking around with it. You might run into the wrong kind of people who want to see if you know how to use it.'

'I already know how. I shot . . . two jackrabbits and a coyote last week. Paw says I'm a dead shot. He says when he rode over to Red Rock, the paper there says you shot down a whole family of killers. He says you're famous because you killed so many people. It that true, Mr Dickson?'

Dickson glanced away, gazing at the

blue silhouette of mountains. 'Papers say all sorts of things. Tell your father not to believe everything he reads. You shouldn't either.'

'Ah . . . I don't know how to read. Paw says book learnin' is only for city folks. He says we're cattle people. We don't need to know how.'

Dickson let the remark pass. Trying to explain anything further was a waste of time. Wild lived in his own small world of ignorance enforced by a father and mother plus four younger sisters all of the same mind.

'I'm gonna go get me that drink now. I never had mescal before.'

'You do that, Zac. But don't drink too much or you'll likely fall off that mule of yours and shoot yourself in the foot, before you get back home.'

The kid stood a moment longer wondering if he was being made fun of. 'Why would I want to shoot myself in the foot, Mr Dickson?'

'Nothing, Zac. It was just a poor joke. Forget about it.'

Wild pushed through the front door as Dickson leaned back, balancing the chair on its back legs, boots propped up on a porch post. No sooner had he gotten comfortable than a new rider came into view, this time the strange figure of a man dressed in a rumpled suit and bowler hat. 'City clothes,' he thought, studying the new arrival pulling to a stop, sweat running down his face red with heat. Lewis Lansing dismounted, holding on to the saddle horn a moment trying to get his breath, balance and composure back.

'I'm praying your name is Benjamin Dickson.' He finally got the words out stepping up on the porch. 'Because if you're not him, I've just come a thousand miles for nothing, and probably lost my job in the process.'

'I'm Dickson,' he nodded. 'Who are you?'

'Thank God for small favours! I'm on my last legs. Do you mind if I pull up a chair and sit? I was just about ready to give up and go back to

Chicago, to resign. I've been trying to find you for nearly a month. My name is Lewis Lansing. I guess that doesn't mean much to you, but I'm a feature writer in Chicago for a very popular men's magazine called the *Gentleman's Gazette*. I don't suppose you ever heard of that, either?'

'No.' Dickson shook his head. 'I don't live in Chicago.' He needled his new guest.

'Yes, I know that. But you might be interested when I tell you why I've come so far to find you. My boss, his name is Horace Throckmorton, owns the *Gazette*. He sent me all the way down here to Arizona to write the story about your life as a famous man tracker, lawman and pistol shot extraordinaire. You know, all those men you shot down face to face? He wants me to put it all down on paper in a brand new book. Your name is already all over popular dime novels back east. We want to write it from the words of the real thing — you. And here's the best part that's going to tickle you. Mr Throckmorton has already given me a signed contract I have right here in my briefcase, that says he'll pay you twenty-five per cent on every novel we sell. You could become a rich man while sitting right here in this chair and never take another step. You don't have to shoot anyone to collect it either!'

Dickson's face grew stone cold. Lansing saw the sudden, chilling change, pulling back in his chair. More sweat began running down his face, soaking his shirt collar.

'You listen to me, and you listen good.' Dickson's answer was short, tense. 'There isn't going to be any book written by me, about me, or any other way. You understand what I'm saying?'

The scribe nodded feebly without speaking, eyes growing wider with fear at the sinister whisper of Dickson's words.

'You print something like that and every two-bit bar fly with a two dollar pistol will try and make a name for himself by shooting me in the back.

This isn't Chicago, so forget the whole idea. I want no part of it!'

Lewis sank back in his chair, lifting the soggy handkerchief again to mop his face. He saw his job, great idea and career sinking fast if he couldn't somehow convince the tall man to change his mind. He desperately tried to think of something else that might work. Suddenly a new idea came to him. He took in a deep breath, girding himself for rejection and more anger.

'Listen Mr Dickson, you have to understand something else I haven't brought up yet. Please hear me out on this. Try to understand that there already are dime novels out using your name. They're all over and you're not making a single red cent out of it. Don't you see they don't need your participation to do that? It's called freedom of the press. They can say or write anything they want, even if it's a pack of lies. For all I know Mr Throckmorton might go ahead and have me write a book about you whether you help me or not. I wouldn't have any say in it at all. Wouldn't it be better if you set the record straight and prove all that other stuff is just hot air? Wouldn't it be more sensible while you're making big money at the same time?'

'No, it would not. You're talking about some stupid book. I'm talking about my life!'

Lansing's shoulders sagged. His head fell and he shook it in defeat. He'd tried everything he could think of. It was clear there was no other way to convince the stubborn man. 'All right, have it your way. I don't have it in me to try and change your mind. I can't leave here today either. I'm too tired to take another stage ride right now. I'll get a room for tonight and try in the morning. Maybe, just maybe, if you have a night to sleep on it you might somehow change your mind and reconsider before I go.'

'I won't. I told you why so don't ask me again. I gambled with my life every time I pulled this six-gun. I'm not going to game with it because of some book.'

13

The rising Arizona sun had barely peeked over the rim of the Rincon Mountains when Lewis Lansing rolled over in his bed for the ten tenthtime, red-eyed from lack of sleep and soaking wet with sweat. Yesterday's sweltering heat had not dissipated overnight. His failure to convince Dickson on a book deal only made sleep more impossible. He envisioned the wrath of his boss when he arrived back in Chicago, chewing him out before firing him in front of all his colleagues. He felt about as low and miserable as he had in all his professional life. His big idea, his dream to do a book about the most famous gunfighter in the west, was over.

The aroma of breakfast cooking downstairs moved him to toss off the sheets. Sitting on the edge of the bed, he tried rubbing the pain out in the back of his neck using both hands. That didn't work either. At least he could try to leave Double Hot on a full stomach, if nothing else. Forcing himself up, he began dressing.

Exiting the room, he was halfway downstairs when he saw Dickson sitting at a table alone, eating in the otherwise empty room. 'Mind if I join you?' He tried to sound positive, forcing a thin smile as he crossed the room.

Dickson looked up, nodding him over. 'Your horse is still outside with the saddle on him. He stayed that way all night. He might be a little ornery to ride once you leave here this morning.'

'Saddled? I wouldn't know how to get it off or put it on. They did that at the ranch for me. You say you have to take them off at night?'

Dickson looked across the table at the greenhorn in dismay. 'You better get back to Chicago. You don't fit too well out here.'

The bartender crossed the room to their table. He was barman, cook and hotel register, all in one. 'What'll you have, Mister?'

'Do you have a menu?'

'Yeah, right here in my head. Breakfast today is javelina and eggs. That's it.'

Lansing stared back at the man with a handlebar moustache, wondering if he was pulling his leg. 'What's a . . . javelina?'

'Wild pig,' Dickson offered. 'This country is full of them.'

'Wild . . . pig?' Lewis's voice trailed off.

'Brush bacon,' the barkeep added, glancing at Dickson with a small smile, enjoying Lansing's obvious discomfort. 'By the way Ben, that kid Zac Wild is sleeping off a big hangover in the back room. He got so drunk last night he couldn't stand up, so I steered him in there. He started getting a little thorny with me. For a while I thought I was going to have to lay him out. Looks like he's going to end up a mean drunk just like his old man, Zink.'

Dickson didn't reply while Lewis was still trying to decide what to do about breakfast.

'I think I'll just have two eggs over easy with toast and butter. Make the coffee black, and hold the pig,' he finally answered.

'We don't have any bread. How about a tortilla instead?'

'What's a tor . . . tilla?'

'Mexican flat bread,' Dickson offered, sipping on his coffee cup.

'Ahh — I think I'll just settle for eggs and coffee. By the way, do you happen to know when the next stage comes through the valley?' He looked up at the barman.

'Usually once every other day or so out of Red Rock, depending on how many paying passengers or freight they have on board. Today might be a good bet.'

Lewis nodded a thank you. 'I'd better eat and get going. I still have to get that knot-headed horse back to the ranch. I don't want to miss that stage or I'll have to stay in this furnace-throated land another day or two. There's no reason for me to suffer any further now.'

Dickson finished breakfast, starting his second cup of coffee, watching the man from Chicago gingerly picking his eggs apart like he expected to find something crawling in them. He was waiting for Lansing to try one more time to convince him to help write his book. Sure enough, when Lewis finished eating he looked up with a hopeful smile. 'Before I go I'd like to bring up one more thing about my offer to you yesterday.'

'Don't waste your time. I already told you the answer is no. You better get going if you want to try to catch that stage.'

'I just wanted to add that my boss, Mr Throckmorton, also authorized me to offer you as much as thirty per cent on those book sales we talked about instead of the twenty-five.'

Dickson leaned forward placing both

hands on the table, staring back at Lewis while trying not to lose his temper, when the door in the back room slowly opened to Zac Wild, leaning on the frame and trying to stay upright. His head felt like it would explode and his stomach churned in sickening revolt. Across the room through fuzzy eyes he saw Dickson sitting at a table with his back to him, talking to another man. He remembered how famous everyone said Dickson was. Even his paw had said so. He also vaguely remembered the remark the tall man made yesterday about falling off his mule shooting himself like a fool. A spark of anger began rising in the kid. Who was Dickson to say he wasn't man enough to hold his liquor or handle a pistol? That was the kind of talk other people in town said when making fun of him and his family because they lived out in the brush and didn't have much. This might be the chance to show all of them how much of a man he really was.

His hand went down for the pistol in his pants top. It wasn't there. Staggering back into the room he found it lying on the bunk. Grabbing it, he struggled to cock the hammer back. Lowering the six-gun behind his back he exited the room, weaving unsteadily toward the two men at the table. As he came up, Lewis looked over Dickson's shoulder seeing the kid suddenly lift the six-gun at arm's length. Before he could yell a warning, a thunderous shot rang out, the .45 caliber bullet smashing into the back of Dickson's head, driving him face down dead on his plate with a round, red-rimmed exit hole in his forehead.

Lansing screamed, trying to push backwards so fast he tipped his chair over, spilling him on to the floor, madly crawling away across the room on his hands and knees. Reaching the wall, he sat up covering his face with both hands, expecting to be shot too.

The barman dove for the shotgun kept under the counter, coming up cocking both hammers back, levelling the deadly scattergun on the kid.

'Drop it Zac, or I'll cut you in two. So help me God, I will!'

Confused, still half drunk, Wild hesitated a moment reeling on his feet, unsure what to do, as the bartender advanced holding the double barrel belt-high, his finger firm on the trigger.

'Don't kill him!' Lewis suddenly yelled. 'Drop the gun, kid. Do what the man says. I . . . I have to talk to you about something. Don't throw your life away now!'

Zac turned toward the scribe and his strange request, still clutching the wheel gun. Suddenly he felt the cold steel of twin barrels pressing into his back. 'I won't tell you again. Let that damn gun fall, or I'll pull off both barrels!' the barman threatened.

'I . . . didn't really mean . . . to do it.' Wild's mouth quivered in regret, struggling to explain the sudden killing, letting the six-gun clatter to the floor.

'What are you going to do with him now?' Lewis questioned, struggling to his feet, crossing the room to look down on Dickson's body. His face twisted in revulsion.

'You have a sheriff or jail?' Lewis asked, unable to stop staring at Dickson's body.

'Hell no, neither one. About all I can do is try to get a marshal over here from Red Rock, to take him in. It's a pretty long ride, but someone has to do it. We've got a telegraph office, though. I'll run down there while you keep this shotgun on him. And we better get some help getting Dickson out of here too. I can't believe this dumb kid actually killed him.'

'I can't hold a shotgun on him. I never handled a gun in my entire life, let alone aimed one at someone,' Lewis pleaded.

'You've got no choice.' He shoved the heavy double barrel into Lewis's hands. 'Just keep it on him and if he tries to run for it, pull off both barrels. I'll be back in a few minutes.'

'Wait a minute. I want to talk to him

before anyone takes him away or puts him in jail,' Lewis protested.

'Talk to him about what? You just saw your friend's brains scattered across this table and you want to talk to him? What kind of a man are you?'

'I'm . . . a writer from Chicago. I came here to talk to Dickson about a book on his life, but now he's dead. This young man, obviously from the wild wood, just killed the most feared and famous gunfighter in the west. His story will make headlines all over this nation.'

'Story? Who cares about that at a time like this! I don't care about any headlines either. You just do what I told you to. I'll be back as fast as I can, and don't let anyone else in here until I am.'

The barkeep disappeared out the door at a run while Lewis turned to Wild, sitting at the table across from the man he'd just murdered. He seemed transfixed on the bloody body as Lansing leaned down talking low and fast, trying to break his trance.

'You listen to me young man, and listen good. I came here to write a book about the man you just murdered, but now I can't. That leaves only you, understand? Now I'll write your story about the struggles and privation you and your family have had to suffer at the hands of people here in Double Hot. I've got some important papers right here in my briefcase, I'll ask you to sign so I can do that story, your story. The money you can earn from it can buy you a top-flight lawyer when they take you to court. Who knows, you might even get off with manslaughter. If you want to make a deal that can save your life, I'll get those papers out right now and have you sign them before anyone else comes in here. What do you say? Are you game for it, Zac Wild? Are you ready for fame and fortune?'

The kid looked up bewildered by the sudden offer. He barely understood what Lansing was even saying, but he knew one thing. 'I . . . I can't write my name.'

'Don't you worry about that one bit. I'll help you. I'll show you where to make your mark. That's all we need for it to be legal. Let's get this deal done and fast.'

Four days later Zac Wild, in handcuffs, was on his way to Red Rock's jail in custody of Sheriff Lane Stokes. Stokes, riding next to Zac on his mule, looked over at the pathetic young man. He couldn't believe someone near idiocy could have ever gotten the drop on Ben Dickson. He knew Dickson well, and of his exploits over the years facing down some of the most dangerous men in Arizona, and everyplace else. It didn't make any sense for him to die by the hands of a teenage kid who could barely get out a complete sentence, yet there it was. He shook his head without comment.

On a small rise not far outside Double Hot, the rock-strewn cemetery overgrown with thorny mesquite and cactus had a fresh mound of calichee with a wooden headboard at one end holding the body of Ben Dickson, bound for eternity. It simply read:

BEN DICKSON
May he at last rest in peace.

Dickson had no wife, family or children to leave behind to mourn him. A handful of local people who knew him got enough money together to buy his simple headboard. Above the boneyard a lone coyote standing on a hill watched the small handful of people beginning to leave. When the last wagon and rider went out of sight, the little brush wolf threw his head back, howling a long drawn-out salute of goodbye, before turning to trot back into brush. It was as good a send-off as the man with a fast gun and no conscience expected to ever get.

On the dusty stage road climbing Mica Mountain, the Canton & Keller four-horse coach rocked to the uneven wheel track while Lewis Lansing sat with his leather briefcase on his lap stuffed full with his fantastic new story about the kid who shot down the most feared gunfighter in the entire west, with only one single shot. He knew his name would be on the lips of every household from the Rocky Mountains to the eastern seaboard when his explosive new novel came out. He even had a title already in mind: 'Ben Dickson, King of Killers'. Even better he no longer had to ask Ben Dickson if he could write it. When the stage crested Ridington Pass, Double Hot went out of sight behind for good. Lewis Lansing had his story. There was no reason for him ever returning. As usual the Arizona sun began its scorching climb up the thermometer, sending that first trickle of hot sweat down the back of his neck, dampening his collar. For the first time since coming to Arizona, a smile of satisfaction and accomplishment lit Lewis Lansing's face. This time he didn't mind the sweat at all.

We do hope that you have enjoyed reading this large print book.

Did you know that all of our titles are available for purchase?

We publish a wide range of high quality large print books including:
Romances, Mysteries, Classics
General Fiction
Non Fiction and Westerns

Special interest titles available in large print are:
The Little Oxford Dictionary
Music Book, Song Book
Hymn Book, Service Book

Also available from us courtesy of Oxford University Press:
Young Readers' Dictionary
(large print edition)
Young Readers' Thesaurus
(large print edition)

For further information or a free brochure, please contact us at:
Ulverscroft Large Print Books Ltd.,
The Green, Bradgate Road, Anstey,
Leicester, LE7 7FU, England.
Tel: (00 44) **0116 236 4325**
Fax: (00 44) **0116 234 0205**

LAND OF THE SAINTS

Jay Clanton

It is the summer of 1858, and the Turner family are making their way along the Oregon Trail to California. The wagon train with which they are travelling is attacked by a band of Paiute, but this is no mere skirmish in the Indian Wars. The territory of Utah, or Deseret as those who live there call it, is in open rebellion against the government in Washington. Turner and his wife and daughter are caught in the crossfire of what is turning out to be a regular shooting war.

FLAME ACROSS THE LAND

Colin Bainbridge

Fark Seaton comes to the aid of old timer Utah Red when he and his flock of sheep are attacked. Who is responsible? The evidence seems to point towards Mitch Montgomery and his Lazy Ladder outfit; but as tension mounts and the bullets fly, Seaton is not so sure. What is the role of Nash Brandon, owner of the Mill Iron? Could Seaton's interest in Montgomery's daughter, Maisie, be clouding his judgement? When the sparks of anger finally blaze into uncontrolled fury, the answers at last begin to emerge.

TO RIDE THE SAVAGE HILLS

Neil Hunter

Arizona, 1888: Marshal Ed Pruitt had been bringing Sam Trask to justice when, following an accident, Trask murdered the driver and escaped. Now Pruitt wants Bodie to bring Trask in before the wanted man can cross the line into Canada. But what should be a straightforward pursuit soon turns into something far more puzzling. Trask is a killer, yet people are willing to cover for him. As he rides the savage hills, facing bullets and treacherous weather, Bodie proves that he's the toughest manhunter the West will ever see . . .

A GUN FOR SHELBY

Jake Henry

1867 and the Civil War was still being fought . . . Forced into taking a job he doesn't want, Savage rides into a desert full of hostile Yavapai Indians to track down a killer. There he is taken captive by a small band of rebels for whom the Civil War has never ended. Although their leader, the legendary General Jo Shelby, now wants to return to Missouri, some under his command would rather see him dead than betray their cause. Can Savage get Shelby home in one piece before the desert is wrenched apart by the explosive fury of the Yavapais?

LONG TRAIL TO REDEMPTION

B. S. Dunn

A U.S. senator and his family have been kidnapped by bandits and imprisoned in the Mexican village of Las Palomas, but the government is reluctant to provoke war by sending troops after them. Joshua Bell of the secret service amasses a team to retrieve the captives: assassin-for-hire Hawk; bounty hunter Wolf McGee; town-tamer Utah Smith; former shootist Walter Cronkite; secret service agent Jess Stuart; and drifter gunfighter Red Kinane. But not all of them can be trusted . . .

SHOWDOWN IN BADLANDS

Businessmen Edward Chambers and Rolo Mackenzie have settled in the mining town of Peralta with the aim of buying up abandoned gold mines to search instead for silver. When the Goss family begins to cause trouble, Rolo and Edward appoint hired gun Ben Dickson as the town's marshal. The Goss boys steal some silver ore and flee to the town of Fool's Gold, and Dickson proves himself ruthless in tracking them down. But the brothers are desperate, and their father is hell-bent on a showdown . . .

SHORTY GUNN

---◆---

SHOWDOWN
IN BADLANDS

Complete and Unabridged

LINFORD
Leicester

First published in Great Britain in 2016 by
Robert Hale Limited
An imprint of The Crowood Press
Wiltshire

First Linford Edition
published 2018
by arrangement with
The Crowood Press
Wiltshire

A catalogue record for this book is available
from the British Library.

ISBN 978–1–4448–3822–0

Published by
F. A. Thorpe (Publishing)
Anstey, Leicestershire

Set by Words & Graphics Ltd.
Anstey, Leicestershire
Printed and bound in Great Britain by
T. J. International Ltd., Padstow, Cornwall

This book is printed on acid-free paper